A TASTE FOR HONEY

H. F. HEARD (1889-1971) was an English social historian, spiritual philosopher, and author of science and mystery fiction. Born in London, he studied at Cambridge University, then turned to writing essays and books on historical, scientific, religious, mystical, cultural, and social subjects, signing them Gerald Heard, the name under which all his non-fiction appeared. He moved to the United States in 1937, accompanied by his friend Aldous Huxley, and soon afterwards founded a college to teach meditation and other spiritual practices. *A Taste for Honey* (1941) was his first foray into fiction, and the character Mr. Mycroft went on to appear in two additional novels by Heard: *Reply Paid* (1942) and *The Notched Hairpin* (1949).

OTTO PENZLER, the creator of American Mystery Classics, is also the founder of the Mysterious Press (1975), a literary crime imprint now associated with Grove/Atlantic; MysteriousPress.com (2011), an electronic-book publishing company; and New York City's Mysterious Bookshop (1979). He has won a Raven, the Ellery Queen Award, two Edgars (for the *Encyclopedia of Mystery and Detection*, 1977, and *The Lineup*, 2010), and lifetime achievement awards from NoirCon and *The Strand Magazine*. He has edited more than 70 anthologies and written extensively about mystery fiction.

A TASTE FOR HONEY

H. F. HEARD

Introduction by
OTTO PENZLER

**AMERICAN
MYSTERY
CLASSICS**

Penzler Publishers
New York

Published in 2019 by Penzler Publishers
58 Warren Street, New York, NY 10007
penzlerpublishers.com

Distributed by W. W. Norton

Cover image: Andy Ross
Cover design: Mauricio Diaz

Paperback ISBN 9781613161210
Hardcover ISBN 9781613161203
eBook ISBN 9781504037761

Library of Congress Control Number: 2018913217

Printed in the United States of America

9 8 7 6 5 4 3 2 1

A TASTE FOR HONEY

To CHRISTOPHER WOOD
A Connoisseur,
This Unclassified Vintage

INTRODUCTION

ATTEMPTING TO combine the mystery novel with other genres is often a risky business that frequently fails, and when it fails, it fails badly. It is common for many of those who are not particularly well-read in the literature of crime to lump it with horror and supernatural literature, ascribing similarities to the two genres that do not exist. The mystery story and the supernatural story not only are not at all similar, they are as diametrically opposed as it is possible to be.

The very essence of mystery and detective fiction is logic and reason, observation and deduction—in other words, ratiocination, to use Edgar Allan Poe's created word. The tale describing supernatural happenings is the 180-degree opposite, with rational thought constantly defied by inexplicable occurrences that have no basis in reasonable expectations.

For a reader to walk in the footsteps of a detective,

searching for evidence, collecting clues, connecting obscure bits of information and forming a rational theory to identify a culprit, is the very heartbeat of a realistic mystery novel. To have the explanation of a mystery come from thin air, to be told that the murder has been committed by a ghost or some other invisible monster, is more than disappointing. It is intolerable.

Having said all that, getting it off my chest, *A Taste for Honey* is not like any book you have ever read. Yes, it is a detective story, and a superb one. But, be warned, there is a hint of something not quite . . . ordinary. No, some unknown power manipulated by a mad scientist who has learned to harness the forces of evil will not play a role here. There is no ghost in sight. It is just that there is a soupcon of uneasiness in realizing that perhaps not everything on Earth is totally comprehensible—including the enormous capacity of some minds to embrace evil.

The author of this classic detective novel, H(enry) F(itzgerald) Heard (1889-1971), was a social historian, spiritual philosopher, and author of occult fantasy and mystery fiction. Born in London, he studied at Cambridge University, graduating with honors in history, then wrote and worked at numerous jobs before becoming a lecturer at Oxford University. He became a fulltime writer of essays and books on historical, scientific, religious, mystical, cultural, and social subjects, signing the works as Gerald Heard—the name under which all his nonfiction appeared; his fiction was published as by H.F. Heard in the United States but under the Gerald Heard byline in England. He wrote hundreds of articles and thirty-five books.

He moved to the United States permanently in 1937, heading a commune in California for many years. He appeared as a character in several Aldous Huxley novels, notably as William Propter, a mystic, in *After Many a Summer Dies the Swan* (1939). He was a noted pacifist who lectured on the subject in America, also speaking on parapsychology; he was a member of the Society for Psychical Research. He had written fourteen non-fiction books on science, civilization, and religion before his first work of fiction, *A Taste for Honey*, was published in 1941.

Mystery readers have recognized *A Taste for Honey* as Heard's masterpiece. The great scholars of detective fiction, Howard Haycraft and Ellery Queen, when they compiled "The Haycraft-Queen Definitive Library of Detective-Crime-Mystery Fiction," included it on their list of the greatest books in the genre.

It is safe to say that no character in fiction has been the subject of more books and stories than Sherlock Holmes. Apart from the sixty canonical stories by Arthur Conan Doyle, there are countless thousands of parodies and pastiches, including a few very good ones, a few decent ones, hundreds of pedestrian ones, and what appears to be an infinite number of abysmal ones. In most cases, readers know that they are holding a Sherlockian story in their hands. It is, after all, why the story was written and why the author felt impelled to use another author's creation for his inspiration.

Things are a little different in *A Taste for Honey*. In it, a tall, slender gentleman called Mr. Mycroft has retired to Sussex to keep bees—just as Sherlock Holmes did. Since Mycroft and Holmes have physical similarities, there has been speculation that Mycroft is actually Holmes, living under an assumed name to assure anonymity. Lending further credence to the theory is that Mycroft is the name of Sherlock Holmes' brother. There are, however, some differences between Holmes and Mr. Mycroft, including the latter's knowledge of and affection for fine food, but readers will certainly recognize the familiar Holmesian voice.

I have given away one of the surprises in the book, though I am confident that the secret has been revealed often enough that few readers will be astounded. The name of the detective is not revealed until the end of the narrative because he has made every attempt to remain anonymous. In an amusing little sketch as the novel reaches its conclusion, when Mr. Mycroft finally reveals his "real" name to both the reader and to the narrator, Sydney Silchester, the man is underwhelmed. He says:

"'You see,' I said, 'now that I do know your real name, I have to own I have never heard of you before.' Then, I must own, he [Mycroft] looked amazed—perhaps the only time I had seen him profoundly surprised, and he turned away without a word."

Sydney Silchester, who tells the story, is a neurotic and mostly unpleasant fellow who has two passions: solitude and honey. He obtains the latter from Mr. and Mrs. Heregrove, the village beekeepers but, when . . . oh, sorry, I can't say more without spoiling at least one surprise.

Silchester has a little more difficulty acquiring the solitude he desires. Isolation, even in a quiet little English village, is difficult to achieve and he finds himself drawn, step by step, into one of the most grotesque and terrifying situations in all detective fiction. His dilemma is made all the more dangerous because, although his life has been directly menaced, he cannot appeal to the police, and neither revolver nor blade could afford him any protection.

Under the circumstances, Silchester is fortunate to be able to put himself under the protection of a man with a brilliant record of circumventing crimes of the most bizarre nature—though nothing in Mycroft's career had prepared him for the resourceful and merciless criminal with whom he now had to deal.

In one of his letters, Raymond Chandler described

meeting Heard and noted that "he wrote a very clever thriller." Christopher Morley, the great Sherlockian and bibliophile, referenced the book when he wrote of the "delight this tale holds for every true detective story lover." The following year, writing again about *A Taste for Honey*, Morley stated that it was "in my own scale of values, the most original and enchanting crime story of last year." Vincent Starrett, the equal of Morley as a learned Sherlockian and bibliophile, averred: "A new volume has been added to the relatively short shelf of detective story classics."

A Taste for Honey was adapted for television in 1955 as an episode of *The Elgin TV Hour* titled *The Sting of Death*. Boris Karloff played Mr. Mycroft. It was also filmed as *The Deadly Bees* as a pure horror film in 1967. The screenplay was by Robert Bloch, who had great respect for the novel and followed the plotline closely. However, the director, Freddie Francis, and the producers, Max J. Rosenberg and Milton Subotsky, wanted a major rewrite and gave the job to Anthony Marriott, whose script bore no relation to the novel—and was execrable to boot. Neither Mr. Mycroft nor Sydney Silchester appear in the film.

Mr. Mycroft appears in two further novels, *Reply Paid* (1942), in which the adventure has moved to California with a murder method equally chilling as that used in the previously volume, and *The Notched Hairpin*

(1949), in which a man has been murdered in a gentle garden by the thrust of a slender instrument identified as an antique hairpin.

The American Mystery Classics series plans to bring back into print the greatest authors and books of the Golden Age of the detective novel. Please look at the back of the book to see other distinguished crime novels.

—OTTO PENZLER

1

THE SOLITARY FLY

SOMEONE HAS said that the countryside is really as grim as any big city. Indeed, I read a novel not long ago that made out every village, however peaceful it looked, to be a little hell of all the seven deadly sins. I thought, myself, that this was rather nonsense—a "write-up"—devised by those authors who come to live out of town and, finding everything so dull, have to make out that there's no end of crime going on just behind every barn door and haystack. But in the last month or so, I'm bound to say I've had to change my mind. Perhaps I have been unfortunate. I don't know. I do know that many people would say that I had been fortunate in one thing: in meeting a very remarkable man. Though I can't help saying that I found him more than a little vain and fanciful and rather exhausting to be with, yet there is no doubt he is a sound fellow to have with one in a tight corner. Though, again, I must say that I think he is more to be valued then, than when things are normal and quiet. Indeed, as I shall show, I am not sure that he did not land me in one trouble in getting me out of another, and so, as I want to be quiet, I have felt compelled, perhaps a trifle discourteously, to refuse to go on with our acquaintanceship.

But I must also own that I did and do admire his skill, courage, and helpfulness. I needed such a striking exception to the ordinary (and very pleasant) indifference of most people, because of the quite unexpected and, I may say, horrible interest that one person suddenly chose to take in me. Yet, as I've said, perhaps I would never have known that I had become of such an awkward interest—the whole thing *might* have passed over without my ever having to be aware of my danger if this same well-meaning helper had not uncovered the pit past which I was unconcernedly strolling. And certainly the uncovering of it led me into great difficulties. I don't like being bothered. I like to think sufficiently well of my neighbors that I can feel sure they won't interfere with me, and I shan't have to do anything to them, and, perhaps I should add, for them. I must be frank, or putting all this down won't get me any further. I suppose—yes, there's no doubt—I came to live in the country because I wanted to be left alone, at peace. And now I have such a problem on my mind—on my conscience! Well, I must set it all down and then, maybe, it will look clearer. Perhaps I'll know what I ought to do. At the worst it can remain as a record after me, to show how little I was really to blame, how, in fact, the whole thing was forced on me.

As I've said, I came to live in the country because I like quiet. I can always entertain myself. When you are as fortunately endowed as that, mentally, and your economic endowment allows you to collect round you the things you need to enjoy yourself—well, then, persons are rather a nuisance. The country is your place and No CALLERS the motto over your door. And I would have been in that happy condition today if I had stuck to my motto. I'm a Jack-of-all-trades, a playboy, if you will. I potter in the garden, though I really hardly know one end of a flower from the other; amuse myself at my carpenter's bench and lathe; repair my grandfather clock when it ails; but fall down rather badly when it comes to dealing with the spring mechanism of the gramophone. I'm no writer, though. I write a neat hand, as I hate slovenliness. But I like playing at making things, not trying to describe them, still less imagining what other people might be thinking and doing.

I have some nice books with good pictures in them. I'm a little interested in architecture, painting, and, indeed, all the arts, and with these fine modern volumes you needn't go traveling all over the place, getting museum feet, art-gallery headache, and sight-seeing indigestion. You can enjoy the reproductions quite as much as the originals when you consider what the originals cost, just to look at, in fatigue and expense. I like turning over the colored plates and photographs of my books in the evening, looking sometimes at a cathedral and then, with only the exertion of turning the page, at the masterpiece of painting which the cathedral contains, but which the photographer was allowed to see in a good light and the visitor is not, and then at an inscription which is quite out of eyeshot of the poor tourist peer he binocularly never so neckbreakingly.

I read a novel now and then, but it must be a nice, easy story with a happy ending. I never wanted to marry; and certainly what I have to tell should be a warning. But I like—or liked, perhaps I should say—to think of people getting on. It made me, I suppose, feel they wouldn't trouble me if they were happy with each other. I suppose I liked life at second hand—reflected, not too real. And certainly, now that it has looked straight at me, I can't say I wasn't right, though I may have been irresponsible.

Well, I mustn't waste more time on myself, though perhaps in a record like this there should be some sort of picture of the man who tells the story and how he came to have to tell it. My name—I believe they always start by asking that—is Sydney Silchester. My age doesn't matter—though I suppose they'd pull *that* out, if they were once on the track of all this; though what difference it makes whether I'm thirty or fifty I can't see. "Of years of discretion," is the description that occurs to me and seems apt. For certainly I am not of years of indiscretion—never, as it happens, was. "Old for his years," they used to say; and now, I believe, young. But am I any longer—"of years of discretion?" Certainly had I been discreet I would somehow not have become involved in all this! But my mind goes round and round like a pet rat in his whirligig. That's because I can't write and also because I am really considerably worried, shocked, and perhaps frightened. Getting it all down, I must repeat, will help. Get it down, then, I will, and no more blundering about as though I were trying to keep something back from someone.

As I've said, it all began through my breaking my rule—the rule, as it happens, of all village life of the better-off, of "keeping myself to myself." It was an accident, in a way, or rather two accidents coming on the top of each other. I'm fond of honey and one of the pleasant things about living in the country is that you can get the real stuff. But what was a little odd in my neighborhood, though I never thought about it, was that practically no one kept bees—said they couldn't make them thrive. Now I wish that I hadn't been so fond of it. Somehow I was too lazy or too busy with other things to try beekeeping myself. That was certainly fortunate. Bees always seemed to me troublesome insects—but how troublesome I never suspected.

I'd found, however, that there was one place where bees were kept and honey for sale, a house toward the end of the village. I found it because it lay on the way to the open country and you needn't go through the main street and run the risk of being stopped and being compulsorily gossiped. I never set out to be a recluse—only just didn't want friends, hadn't time for them. The couple who lived up there seemed quite as uninclined to make a small business transaction into a bridgehead for talk leading to a call. That seemed to me to be a distinct additional find. They were a Mr. and Mrs. Heregrove. When I called for my monthly supply, sometimes I saw one, sometimes the other. It wasn't a very small place, but they, too, never seemed to entertain. For all I know, they ran the house, gardens, and paddock themselves. They may have had a servant the first few times I called. Certainly I never saw anyone but themselves about the place later. If I had wanted to make friends they were hardly the people I would have chosen. I hate untidiness.

I saw Mrs. Heregrove first—or, to be quite exact, heard her before I saw either her or her husband. She had an unpleasantly penetrating voice and she was using it with such effect that she herself was evidently quite unable to hear the rusty doorbell I was ringing. Eavesdropping has never appealed to me. Other people's affairs always appear quite dull enough when one has to be told them and is expected to sympathize. I keep what little patience I have for such occasions. So when for the third time the unpleasant voice had asked of what was clearly a tense and provocative silence, What he meant to do about it and whether he was going to live on her money until they both starved, as the question was certainly not for me to answer or to hear, I rapped sharply with my stick on the door. That brought immediate silence, and a few seconds later the voice's face was before me. They matched.

"Well?" she said, with sharp suspicion.

"I want to buy some of your honey," I said at once. I was amused at the quickness with which the face changed, and the voice, too.

"Certainly; I have it both in comb and in jars."

I lay in a month's supply at a time. I also always pay cash—hate bills. I told the woman I'd take half a dozen combs and six jars and took out my purse to pay. She altered even more rapidly. I couldn't help noticing that the face became so lit with relief as to become actually good-looking. She hurried indoors and I caught sight of a shabby hall. In a few minutes she was back with the combs and the jars.

"I could lend you a basket to carry it," she said, and brought a large wicker thing mended with string.

"Thanks," I quickly countered. "I'll bring it back when passing again."

I feared she might make the retrieving of the basket an excuse for a call; at the best a bore, at the worst a beg.

But she replied, "Please do, and perhaps you'll be needing more honey or could recommend mine to your friends."

That was our first meeting. I did bring back the basket and got a second supply, and, as one is a creature of habit, one took to going up there as a matter of course. I never heard them quarreling again.

Once while I waited I caught sight of Heregrove himself. He turned and looked at me. Didn't nod indeed, he appeared quite suspicious and unfriendly, although he must have seen me at the door plenty of times. I said nothing and he turned to go down the path, with his head bent, through the garden, which I noticed again was badly neglected. I watched him go out at the upper end and cross the paddock. There were some tumble-down stables shutting in that side of the field. I had been quite sure that the Heregroves didn't use them, but today I noticed that there was a horse in one of the stalls. Heregrove swung open the half door and disappeared inside. At that moment his wife came out to me with my order of honey. I remember distinctly turning over in my mind their having bought a horse. They had no trap, indeed, they were seldom seen outside their grounds. They clearly didn't like going into the village—owed bills, I suspected.

Then the tragedy happened. I was just running out of honey and was thinking of going up for more, in a day or two. The girl who cleans the house for me, who is a good worker and whose flowing tongue I had thought my icy silences had at last frozen up for a long winter of my content, began to trickle.

"Your honey nearly gone, sir."

I knew this was an opening. I plugged it unwisely with, "Well, I always order it myself, Alice."

"I know, sir." (I saw I had somehow opened the dam, not closed it.) "You always gets it at pore, dear Mrs. Heregrove's."

I recognized that "pore-dear" at once. It can only be used, like the Greek "beautiful and good," as a sort of Siamese-twin epithet; it means, of course, that the recipient is dead. I must have shown a flicker of interest or surprise. My enemy rose like a subarctic river in the spring.

"Not that the village c'd ever think much of either of them. Coming here and giving airs and then running bills and never paying. But, Lor, they was right out of heels, as you might say."

"I wouldn't," I interposed. "I don't want—"

But my wishes, commonly law, were now only the

wishes of the living against the ancient right to proclaim the dead. The flow ran on.

"And that Heregrove: you could hardly call him 'mister' at the best. She was a lydy come down, but he—well, my dad said he never heard a fuller tongue, no, not in a barman. He'd spent all her money, they say, before the end. Why she'd ever 'a' married him no one ever could think, but parson was once heard to say that Heregrove had been a scholar of some sort and lydies are often queer-like, in that way—take a brain which can't even pay its way and let a figure go which c'd at least serve them—"

Alice saw that her tongue had got its head and was itself not only wandering but had reached the verge of "unlydylikeness." But with a magnificent pull she brought herself out of the tailspin, and before I could claim sanctuary of shocked bachelorhood, zoomed on. Mixed metaphors, I suppose—but an excited and talking woman seems to me to combine the characteristics of all the violent and rapid forces of nature and man. She zoomed into the vasty halls of death.

"Well, she's gone, and taken in the strangest way. Perhaps he'll feel it's a judgment on him, but none can say for sure. But we're all sorry now for her, pore dear lydy. Mrs. Brown, who has laid out 'undreds, you might say, and says she likes the doing of it, says it's a sweeter job any day than Miss Smith's, the monthly, for when we come we're all of a mess and go on giving trouble and needing to be changed, but when we go, we go quiet, don't mess our clothes, and can be laid so we look like statutes—Mrs. Brown says it was just a terrible sight, she—pore, dear Mrs. Heregrove—was that swollen and black. And she's right, for I asked Mrs. B. if I might have a look. Heregrove had taken himself off after calling and seeing Dr. Able—"

At that I did break in.

"Alice," I nearly shouted, "did Mrs. Heregrove die of something infectious? If so—" I said, drawing back and pulling out my handkerchief.

"Bless you, no, sir. She was as healthy as you nor me last night. She didn't die of a sickness. She died of a haccident, of stings. The bees got her. Though why, considering she'd been quite one of them for so long—but, then, you'd never know. My uncle—"

The main wave was past; the news was out. Only an ever-widening ripple of reminiscence would follow.

I turned to the garden door, saying over my shoulder, "When you have laid lunch you needn't wait," and myself waited for no more.

Still Mrs. Heregrove's strange end stuck in my mind, even though it wasn't infectious, and kept on passing through my thoughts as I occupied myself at various jobs. I've said I know little about bees but of course I knew they could, like most spinsters in crowds, become at moments temperamental and even neurotic. Perhaps that was one reason why I never had kept them. And now I would have to find another source of honey. Heregrove would have to destroy his lot. Even if he stayed on in the village he could hardly go on beekeeping. They'd be dangerous to him, no doubt, and hardly anyone would like honey manufactured by a homicidal horde. Probably even to call at the house would be to risk attack. I felt a strong distaste to being stung to death or going at all near where such a fate could possibly fly upon me.

The question was in my mind for some days, partly because at every meal I was reminded of it by seeing my honey stock run lower and partly because when I went to do shopping in the village I couldn't avoid hearing— like a sort of Handel chorus—the same phrases over and over again till I had the whole story. Ours is a compact little village, almost a townlet, so you can get most of the things you want and, indeed, quite a number I've no wish for. So I can do most of my shopping without having to send away for things. The story interlined my own business questions and answers.

"Dr. Able knew a case just like that before." "Dr. Able and the coroner talked it over in court." "Heregrove said the bees had been cross and quarrelsome with him lately and he'd told his wife." "The coroner said it was a plain, sad case, an accident." "The coroner said the bees should be destroyed and Heregrove said he'd be doing that anyhow."

Well, that settled my concern, such as it was. I'd have to find another supply-source. That led to the second accident, my second honey hazard, which I now see was needed to bring the first, which I had already taken quite unconsciously, into play.

2

THE NEW BEEKEEPER

I HAD to find another honey seller. Beekeepers were evidently very scarce, though I did not know how scarce. And, further, my dread of business dealings leading, if made with amateurs, to social entanglements, meant that I couldn't seek in the village itself asking all and sundry if any hive fanciers were known. I was determined to find a retailer who would not involve me in village life. And luck, as I thought, came my way at my first cast. But luck is a neutral word; it can be bad, just as well as good. This, after all, was bad. But perhaps I'd better leave luck alone. I don't like the word much. It has a superstitious flavor and I'm just superstitious enough, and clever enough, to know what a lot we don't know, and to leave superstitions severely alone. I'm not yet out of this wood or I wouldn't be so carefully retracing my steps in this account. Heaven only knows where it may all end. So

I'll be cautious and say it was Destiny which took me along Waller's Lane.

It's a pretty walk, anyhow, and one of the least frequented. There are one or two houses along it, but they stand so well back and are so well screened that you would hardly notice them. I never had, beyond being vaguely aware that there must be some dwellings thereabouts. You couldn't avoid knowing that, for a small gate or two open through the high overgrown hedges here and there. I was wandering along, so much enjoying the quiet that I'd forgotten any purpose in my walk but the pleasure of taking it. For the lane dips after half a mile and there you are in a mossy sunken road which at that time of year, full summer, is like a garden. I don't care for big views. They somehow make me yawn. Perhaps I'm not long-sighted enough. But high, sloping banks covered with flowering wild plants seem to me the best possible scenery. Just at the right range, changing all the time and at the right angle.

I had, as it happened, actually stopped to look at half a dozen uncommonly tall snapdragon spires in full bloom, when, following their stalks to the top, my eye was caught by something beyond and above them. It was a small notice poking its head through the hedge at the bank's top. Seeing it, I noticed that there was a footpath gate beside it. The lettering of the notice was too small for me to read from where I stood, so, almost involuntarily, I mounted the steps which I found set in tussocks of grass. It was with nothing but amusement and pleasure, with no foreboding at all, that I read in quite beautifully spaced and shaped Roman letters: "The Proprietor has at present a certain amount of surplus honey of which he would be willing to dispose."

I think I've said that, although I'm not a writer and correspond as little as possible, I rather pride myself on my calligraphy. A scrambling age sees no discourtesy in illegibility and no gain in penmanship. But I do. I saw at a glance that the hand that wrote that notice saw more in handwriting than the surface sense of the words. "The style is the man"; very well, the hand is the gentleman. The lettering was, as all notices should be, based on the incomparable capitals of the Trajan Column, but anyone whose "caps" were so sensitive and whose serifs so assured would certainly command, I thought, an excellent italic. Then there was the intriguing fact that a notice, written with such care, should be posted in a moss-grown lane and, moreover, almost out of sight. And, finally, here was my honey—a supply as sequestered as I could require.

Three things like these coming together are some explanation—if the whole thing seems inexcusable—for my unprecedented precipitancy. Almost without reflecting what reception I might meet and what involvements I might incur, I lifted the latch, walked up a path which wound through a hazel thicket, and suddenly found myself, to quote "poor, dear" Mr. Yeats, in a "bee-loud glade." A lawn on three sides had dense herbaceous borders sloping up to thick yew hedges, over the top of which a fringe of hazel sprays could be seen. On the fourth side the lawn ended in a low white house with french windows opening onto the grass.

On the lawn itself, in tidy ranks, stood those miniature Swiss chalets which have taken the place of the romantic but I understand insanitary skep. The air was dense with the chalets' population. After our village tragedy, I stood with some apprehension wondering where these queer socialists might rule that trespass began, honey-making must stop, and all workers must unite to attack the exploiter. I was keeping my eye so carefully cocked to judge whether an air attack might be impending that I started with surprise when a quiet voice at my elbow remarked, "They are not militant workers, these. I get quite good enough results up till now, at least for my purposes, from the Dutch queens, so I don't continually disturb the poor things' temperament. They are nervous enough anyhow, without making them more excitable with Italian blood."

I turned to see beside me a serene face, a sort of unpolitical Dante, if I may so put it and not seem highbrow. It was cold, perhaps; or maybe it would be juster to say it was super-cooled, cooled by thought until the moods and passions which in most of us are liquid or even gaseous had become set and solid—a face which might care little for public opinion but much for its opinion of itself.

But I mustn't run on like this. I expect it is the fault of a bad writer—can't keep down to facts. Perhaps I didn't notice all this at once. But I was impressed, I know, because I remember saying to myself, "How like Dante," and then having to check myself (for my mind is always flighty, as anyone will see who has got as far as this) because I began to speculate whether if Dante were reincarnated today what he would do to get in his visit to Hell. Where would he find the cave opening? In modern war, maybe, or in a city slum, but hardly in the country or in a village.

"You are my first purchaser," he went on, evidently seeing that my mind was wandering and wishing to put me at my ease. "It is good of you to walk over so far from your place—"

"You know me, then?" I interrupted. "I don't go much into the village and have no friends there and don't remember catching sight of your face. You are a newcomer, aren't you? I often come down the lane but don't remember seeing before the notice which explains my call."

"No one else has," he replied. "It has been there a little while and considerable numbers of the village 'quality' have come down the lane, but none has troubled to go up the steps to see what is written on it."

That remark surprised me. It seemed out of character, somehow. I couldn't resist, therefore, saying, though it was perhaps a little impertinent, "You keep as close a watch on your lane and your notice as a fisherman on his stream and float."

"In a way, yes and no," he smiled, evidently not at all put out by my personal remark.

I thought, however, that it would be polite to put myself back into the picture.

"You come up to our end of the village and have seen my house?" I questioned.

"I must confess, no," he answered, again smiling. "You see," he added, "I have been busy settling in for some time and, like yourself, my reason for coming to the country was not for company but to be busy with all these incessant interests which the town, with its distractions, never really tolerates."

"But how, then—"

"Well," he kindly forestalled me, "there are so many ways of being wise after the event that I have sometimes thought during my life that if we would only act on that rather despised motto we would need to ask far fewer questions—which you and I agree are always, if only the slightest, infringement of that privacy we both prize so highly."

I could not help smiling at the way he had read my thoughts and he smiled, at least with the muscles round his keen eyes if not with his thin lips.

"No one," he continued, "who has taken some little care not to disregard things can fail to notice how much of our past and our settled environment we carry about with us wherever we go. I'm not a geologist, but soils always repay a little attention. This village, like many another in England, is a jigsaw puzzle of earths. That, by the way, tells us something about the past. Our ancestors planted these settlements in order to live off the soil, not to retire from town. So there have to be water and woodland and tilth: woods for fuel and the hogs' pfannage; good soil for harvests and, above all, good water. To get all that means living where the layers of soil have been cut by water so as to give man a selvaged slice of each of the qualities he wants.

"Now you live up at what was the clay end of the village. I'm nearer the light heath soil. You have tiny patches of dried clay on your trousers. One clue helps another. I probably should not have been able to pick up that first clue which tells me where you live if it had not been able to give me the second indication—that you live alone and don't like being looked after too rigorously—in fact, can entertain yourself best when alone."

"But why—"

"The notice," he intervened, "which is well written,

asking the passer-by to purchase and yet put just out of ordinary eye-range? An experiment. Village life, we agree, is a problem. Free, yes, but apt to lose its freedom even more quickly than town. A researcher does not need absolute solitude. Indeed, when I was working, I often found that it helped to talk over a problem with an interested if less absorbed mind. Some steps of reasoning can be run through and checked more quickly in speech than by writing them down, and often the listener, however inexpert, will see a slip oneself has overlooked."

A curiously simple and neat Naturally Selective trap, I thought.

"You'll be thinking I treat my neighbors as prey and you sprung the gin. But I may want help on a problem which should interest the right man as much as it intrigues me. I'm not an apiarist and don't want to meet such specialists. You remember Henry Ford's dictum: 'A specialist is someone who is always telling you what can't be done.' In pure, as well as in applied science, I have found that to be true—someone who tells you that it has all been found out, that there is no further mystery, there is nothing more to discover."

"You're doing research in bees," I interrupted, "but I only want to eat their honey!"

"You shall; but hear me out. Then, if you become my customer and not my acquaintance, I can have the parcel of honey left on you regularly and you need not risk any further conversation. I came down here to study bees. Honey to me is simply a by-product I must dispose of. I'm not a Maeterlinckist! I believe he greatly overrates the intelligence of bees. Anyhow, I'm not interested in what intelligence they may have. All my life I have been estimating human intelligence not by its books or words but by its tracks. Now I want to study something else, but still by its tracks. I want to know about bees' reactions. After all, they are social beings given to living in dense towns. But, though like us, how different! There are no end of problems to be studied. There are the particular flowers they go to, the peculiar vision they have so as to pick out such blooms, and so the particular sort of honey they yield. We might get special brands of honey from certain broods—"

I was faintly interested, but began to feel much more strongly that I wanted to get my honey and get away.

"Yes," I said vaguely. "I expect a market could be found for super-honey just as for special proprietary jams and marmalades."

He saw my restlessness.

"If you will step inside I will make up a parcel for you," he remarked, leading me toward the house.

We entered a room on the left of the hall. It was evidently his laboratory.

"I will bring you the combs and the jars in a moment," he said. "I apologize for boring you. Yes, yes, and it was not—I must again beg your pardon—unintentional. You remember Oscar Wilde's silly remark, 'A gentleman is one who is never rude unintentionally?' I think, however, it may be more truly said that a trained mind is one which never bores unintentionally."

The boredom which had been growing vanished, and again I felt a not altogether pleasant surprise. One gets stiff when faintly startled.

"I'm afraid I don't quite understand, Mr.—?"

"Mycroft, if you will," he answered, with that quiet smile of his which was certainly disarming. "The truth is," he added, "I did first put up my notice as a sort of wager with myself as to whether in this village I should find a fellow curioso—not a specialist, not a conventionalist. I own I discovered, almost before you did, that I had lost my bet."

"Why, then," I acidly remarked, "did you continue?"

"Please step over here," came the quick reply, almost an order. He was standing with his hand on a downturned glass bell jar. It covered a square of white paper on which lay a small object. The step I took, almost involuntarily at his command, brought me where I could see what it was.

"A dead bee?" I asked, somewhat challengingly. He lifted the glass bulb and handed me a large magnifying glass. As soon as I took it, with a pair of forceps, he lifted another dead bee off the window sill and placed it beside the first on the square of paper.

"Would you, please, examine these two bodies through the lens?"

"They don't look very different to me," I was just replying, when under the lens a forceps point advanced and pressed on the abdomen of one of the dead bees. The body cockled a little and quite clearly the saber-curved sting was thrust out, and retracted as soon as the pressure was released. Before I could ask what such an unilluminating experiment showed, however, the forceps point darted onto the abdomen of the second bee, depressed it in the same way, and out came the sting—but what a sting! It curved round until it seemed it would pierce through the chitin mail of the dead insect's own thorax.

The voice at my shoulder said, "There's a pretty problem here. The last is, of course, an Italian—fierce bees, anyhow, but I think, from comparing the body with some care with standard Italians, that this is a special variety. Certainly it was psychologically remarkable, even if the rest of it, except for that sting, is physiologically normal. It had the temper of a hornet. It attacked until it was killed. Of course, it came in a troop, so I dissected a number of them. They all had these super-stings. That was remarkable enough to an amateur apiarist; but what was even more remarkable was the result of a small biochemical experiment."

Turning to a shelf, he took out of a rack a glass phial not thicker than a knitting needle.

"There are hardly half a dozen drops of venom in this tube," he remarked. "I have had to gather it from the stings of these bees. Perhaps I would have overlooked the necessity of doing so if it had not been that when my colonies were attacked—when I saw what was on, I myself donned bee-veils and gloves and got ready to defend myself with a special bee-smoker—my poor mastiff ran out. The invaders were not really attending to us, any more than we human beings, in a battle, waste our ammunition on the crows and vultures. But one of these miniature monsters swooped past us, caught the dog's smell, dived, struck, and my poor Rollo gave one howl and fell over. He struggled for some time when I carried him inside. I thought a camphor injection was going to bring him through, though his pain was obviously so great that I thought of putting a bullet in his brain if it did not cease. But suddenly rigors seized him, his tongue lolled out, and he was dead.

"I have had the opportunity of studying toxicology for some years. The only venom I can compare this with in strength—though, of course, its chemical base is the formic acids group—is the incomparably virulent secretion of two spiders—the small yellow which is found in northern Queensland and the so-called black widow of southern California. Even the giant ant lately found in Guiana, Paraponera Clavata, though one sting of it can paralyze a limb for some hours, does not approach the toxicity of this poison."

"But," I said, "what does all this mean?"

I felt, rather than fully recognized, a growing sinisterness in the atmosphere. I wanted to get away, wished I'd never come, but felt somehow that to go off now with the problem all vague and pervasive was only to carry it with me, like a swarm of bees trailing a man who can't shake them off his track! His next words confirmed my doubts and made my misgivings all too unpleasantly definite.

"I told you I put up my notice because, first, I wanted to carry out a casual experiment in seeing whether I could select a possible confrère, and then, after I had a more remarkable visit than I had counted on by what I think I may call in every sense of the word inhuman visitors, I saw I must signal for someone who had two characteristics—that he was a bit of a recluse, so that he might not gossip about what even then seemed as though it might turn out to be a business both ugly and easily driven out of reach, and also that he was a honey lover."

"Why the honey part?" I said, rather feebly and vaguely. My whole thought was bent on the unpleasant realization of how, like a fly limed on flypaper, I was getting every moment more firmly embedded in this beastly business.

"Because you certainly have noticed that the Heregroves were the only people who sold honey in this place. They may not do well. It is hardly a millionaire's occupation, but they have had no other. So anyone who was a honey fancier and so would not buy the shop's stuff, could tell me about the Heregroves, for he would certainly be their customer."

"But why couldn't you call yourself," I asked with weak irritation, "or go openly into the village and inquire about the Heregroves? Why all this hokey-pokey and setting little traps for the innocent curious?"

I tried to make my remarks sound jocular, but the truth is that I was wanting to be as rude as I could with safety, for I was rapidly getting cross over the whole thing and, what was worse, felt that after being cross I might find that I had reason to be frightened. So I added, to smooth things over a bit, "Though I must own the trap has done its work neatly enough."

He smiled again kindly. There could be no doubt of that, and I could not help feeling that if I had to get into a mess with other people's business it might be hard to imagine a stronger and more capable man with whom to face a storm. Even now I still wish that I had kept clear of it all—but there's Destiny, of course, as I've already said.

"Don't say trap. Say my S.O.S. to which you have most generously responded." His voice was equally reassuring. "I couldn't go asking questions in the village because that might rouse suspicion and would certainly have brought me, whether or no correct information, undesirable allies."

Somehow I felt a certain quite unreasonable reassurance at being called by implication a desirable ally, though all that it really meant was that I was getting still more committed to schemes I did not understand and did most actively, if vainly, suspect.

"To visit the Heregroves themselves was, of course, out of the question, even more than making inquiries about them in the village. It is quite clear what he or they have done; though I must say it is so startling that it has shocked me back to a line of thought which I had told myself I had left for good. Heregrove has bred a bee to put all other beekeepers out of business. I confess it is an ingenious notion. I've confirmed it, though. I've already found that up till a few years ago there was quite a lot of beekeeping in this district. Now, as you know, you can't get honey anywhere locally."

"But," I broke in—for I must own my interest in this extraordinary story was getting the better of my self-concern, the whole tale was so mad, bad, and ridiculous—"but what an absurd amount of energy and ingenuity to spend just to corner the honey market of Ashton Clearwater."

"Yes, I thought that, too, and it puzzled me," he replied. "Of course, inventors are kittle cattle. For the sake of an experiment they'll ruin themselves, and to make a discovery they'll risk any number of people's lives, their own included. Still it puzzled me. Of course, after the attack on my hives I realized that a thing like this could and pretty certainly would grow. Apiarists are not used to suspecting people. Heregrove may have lit on this thing as a pure researcher and then have hunted about to see how he could make it pay. His super-bee may, indeed, have acted like a Renaissance 'bravo' or a Frankenstein's monster and gone off killing on its own. That may have put the idea into his head. 'Oh, Opportunity, thy guilt is great. 'Tis thou—'"

"Please," I said, "I prefer at this point psychology to poetry and facts to anything."

"Well," he smiled, "I can tell you the Heregrove bees came literally out of the blue. Fortunately they are so stupid that even if he did send them specifically they could not tell him that their expedition of extermination had failed."

"How did it fail? How could it?" I exclaimed.

"You want only facts," he chuckled, "and no theories. That, of course, is not possible if you wish to understand. But the fact remains, as your ears and eyes tell you, the home team survived."

"Then," I said, with a sigh of relief, "they are not so deadly as we feared."

"Oh, yes, they are," he answered, quietly. "I told you I drove off the first attack from myself and when my poor Rollo was dead and I could do no more for him, I decided to see if I could save at least my bees. Wrapped in bee-veils and gloves, I charged the smoke-thrower with a peculiarly strong smoke I used once when I was attacked long ago in not dissimilar circumstances: what I then took to be an accident but now suspect was a similar discovery being used by a man not unlike our present customer. Discoveries are generally made twice over and often fall into undesirable hands and even come into undesirable brains."

"But was the smoke enough?"

I wanted him to get on. Age and a long-practiced calm had made him more willing to view the past as equally interesting as the present than was I. I had spoiled my walk, missed my lunch, and had not even secured my honey. As a matter of fact, I was only staying on until I could learn how safe it was to go. I had no intention of leaving if there was any chance that in a quiet bend of the lane there might be a sudden hum and before one could even cover one's face one would be pricked to death with red-hot knitting needles. But I had no intention of staying, wasting more of my time, the moment I could be sure that the coast (or rather the sky) was clear.

"Yes, yes, the smoke worked. I mightn't be here if it

hadn't. One crept up my leg and I smoked it only just in time. They're so devoted they'd work their way through anything. I doubt that gloves would be much protection for long against those super-stings. They are prodigious fighters, even normal bees. We'd have had no chance if they had been even a fifth our size."

He saw my dulling eye, went over to the door, and called out, "Mrs. Simpkins, please lay another place and call us as soon as lunch is ready." He turned back to me. "You will stay, won't you? Indeed, I don't want to be an alarmist, but I think you had better. I agree I have taken long in telling you how the land lies but cases such as these I have found can only be grasped—and caught" (he added after a pause) "if one understands much detail which at first sight seems irrelevant."

From the back of the house I heard wheezing but quite reassuring complaints.

"Lunch as soon as it's ready! And it's ready and bin ready this twenty minute and mor'n. Well, there's the bit of cold salmond. An' the patridge pie's warmed up none too bad. Couldn't have kept it waiting yesterday but today it's taken it nicely. Cold gooseberry tart with the whipped cream—never expected it to whip today—"

The inventory was as good to my eye as to my ear and even better on the tongue. My host knew about food and also about wine. He talked both, well and fully, as if he wouldn't touch on shop at mealtimes. I was hun-

gry at first, fell to, and fell in with his mood. But toward
the end it struck me that it was a grim little meal, really. Here was I with an unknown man who had already
dropped a number of most sinister hints and had shown
me also in the other room enough venom to make me
die in agony in less than a minute—and, what's more,
for the coroner's inquest to dismiss my death as though
I had been only bitten by a flea and taken it badly. It was
the thought of the coroner which made me push back
my plate.

"If you have finished," my host said, rising, "I won't
detain you for more than a few moments longer. We
should, however, finish our discussion," he added, dropping his voice, "out of the range of any easily frightened
ears."

Again I felt that queer, irrational disturbance when
pleasure at flattery is mixed with misgiving as to the
flattery's motive. I was already alarmed and had good
reason to be. However, I repeated to myself: "Better
know the worst; ostrich tactics are little use when you
may be fatally stung in the back."

3

ROLANDING THE OLIVER

"Briefly," said my host, when we were once more seated in the laboratory, with the phials and the dead bees to lend point to his words, "the more I thought over Heregrove's work, the more I was sure he had more or less blundered on this discovery while experimenting with bee-breeding."

"But how did you beat off the attack of his bees? Didn't they come back?"

"Yes, but by that time I was ready for them. That is why I think—deduction, I fear, yet often all we have—" (he chuckled rallyingly at me, and I feared a relapse into the past or, worse, into theorizing), "I think Heregrove doesn't know much about bees except their biology. Anyhow, I thought he didn't know much about bee psychology, about their patterns of behavior; though I'm not so sure even of that, now. It is pretty certain, though, that he didn't know that there is an answer to his pirate bee.

"I told you I was more interested in my bees themselves than in their honey. Come into my library a moment. I can best show you there. An actual illustration," he added, gauging my impatience, "often saves time," and then, with a glint of superiority which made me obey because I hate any unpleasantness, "especially when a mind, unfamiliar with a strange fact, must understand it unmistakably!"

By the window in the library hung a cage with a couple of small birds in it. I was going to walk in and take a chair, for I had been quite uncomfortably perched on a bench all the while in the laboratory, but suddenly my shoulder was held.

"Don't move," whispered my queer beekeeper. "Look at the birds and don't speak loudly."

"What am I to notice?" I muttered back, more crossly even than I had meant. All these antics vexed me.

"You notice nothing?" went on the level whisper. "Even when your attention is drawn to it?"

"I see two small birds," I whispered back, playing perforce this ridiculous game. "And one is sitting on the upper perch and the other on the lower."

Then the absurdity of being made to take part in an intelligence test like a backward schoolchild, by a perfect stranger, irritated me so that I wouldn't any longer go on whispering.

Aloud I asked, "Would you be good enough to tell

me what we are looking at and what it is meant to convey?"

"Well, anyhow, that remark of yours has ended the performance," he replied airily. "And, for clues: the familiar passage, 'Look how the heavens' down to 'muddied vesture of decay' from *The Merchant of Venice*, contains the explanation." Then, seeing that my irritation was really mastering me, he stopped smiling and added, "Sir, you must pardon an old man. It is not senility, though, but something almost as out of date—patient thoroughness. When we entered, those birds were singing. At least one of them—the male, of course—was performing and the female was listening enraptured. No, you are not deaf—only a little unobservant with your eyes. One can see his throat swell and his beak open. No human ear—you get my Shakespearean quotation?—can catch one of those notes which his mate so appreciates."

"Yes, Mr. Mycroft, yes," I said, a little mollified (for it was a queer fact of which I had never heard before and I like queer facts). "But what have these birds to do with the bees? Are they to charm away the pirates?"

"You are pretty close to the truth," he replied, surprisingly.

"How on earth can a bird we can't hear, sing away a bee which is probably deaf? I've heard of bee-catching birds but—"

"We don't know of any bird as yet which can serve

this purpose, but this inaudible songster was unknown to our grandparents. And we now know of a spellbinding singer which can do what you ask. More remarkable than a bird: it is actually a moth, a moth which sings a humanly inaudible note! I had to show you the birds because experimenting with them gave me a piece of apparatus which may be of no little use to both of us. They gave me my first records. When I had learned how to make these, and the hen bird had kindly shown me by her absorbed attention that I had indeed caught the note, I then went on to the harder task of recording a far more difficult voice and trying it out on a far more difficult and awkward audience."

We had gone back to the library. Mr. Mycroft, making me, I must confess, catch something of his interest—for I'm interested in gadgets—took out from an upper shelf what looked like a small homemade gramophone combined with a barograph. The drum had on it fuzzy lines like those I once saw on an earthquake chart. Beside the drum was a small hollow rod the use of which I couldn't imagine. He started the machine and the fine pen began its rapid scrawling on the paper as the drum slowly revolved.

"You are now listening to one of the most magical voices in the world," remarked Mr. Mycroft, complacently.

"You can say so," I replied, somewhat tartly. "But as

you like quotations as clues to opinions, I can give you one from Hans Andersen's Magic Weavers: "'The King hasn't got any clothes on at all,' cried the child.'"

"Dickens will do as well," he chuckled. "'There ain't no such person as Mrs. Harris.' But there is a voice, even if, I regret to say, only a potted one, singing in this room so long as that needle pen trembles. Look."

He threw open a panel in the outside wall and revealed the back of a glass hive in which the bees could be seen thickly crawling over the layers of comb. Stepping back, he swung the horn of the gramophone until it was trained on the glass panel in the wall. In two strides he was back again. With a single movement, the sheet of glass was swung back, the comb exposed to the air. We heard the industrious hum rise to an angry buzz of protest. I was about to make for the door when the buzz was cut short even more swiftly than it had arisen. Not, though, to sink back into the contented working hum. What is more, complete stillness held the hive. It was a bee version of the Sleeping Beauty's castle. Mr. Mycroft's hand stretched back. The whirring stopped and, with the last scratch of the pen, the hive came again to life. For a second the bees hesitated, like an audience just before it breaks out of its spell into applause. I did not, however, wait for their ovation. Without asking leave, I clapped shut the glass wall. In a few moments they were as busy as ever on their obsessing honey.

"You could have waited a little longer," Mr. Mycroft remarked. "They are so dazed that they generally go straight back to work—work, for all workers, is the best escape from unpleasant questions and baffling experiences. Well, that is how I routed the invaders. We have air detectors against planes, but we have yet to find a note which will make enemy pilots forget they came to bomb us. When Heregrove's bees came back, I was ready with my bell-mouthed sound muskets turned to the sky. Down they swooped. As soon as they were in range—which I had found by experimenting with my own bees—I started up my inaudible order to desist. 'Heard melodies are sweet but those unheard are sweeter,' certainly if they save your hives. Already my bees and the invaders were fighting, but, at the first needle scratch on the drum, I saw them fall apart. My own dropped down to their alighting boards. Of the enemy, some lit on the flowers and trees; others settled on the lawn. It was then that I picked up enough specimens to make all the tests which I've shown you."

"One moment," I said. Up to that time I had stood like an open-mouthed simpleton being shown an invention which might be magic or might be normal mechanism, for all he could decide. But now I was on my own ground or at least not far from it. "One moment. Isn't there something wrong about all this? I'm rather interested in gramophones in my way and I sometimes read about them. I've understood that the best gramophone today will not record even the highest note audible to the fully hearing human ear. How about these super-notes?"

"I'm glad you know about these matters," he replied, "for it makes it more interesting for me to describe to you this ingenious little toy. Perhaps you know that Galton made a whistle which blows a note which we can't hear but a dog will. That whistle set me on this line of research. You see the principle incorporated in that hollow rod on the far side of the machine by the drum. I won't go into details, but what happens is that air vibrations too fine and high for the ordinary gramophone recording or disk to render are stepped down when we are recording and then, through this simple but ingenious mechanism, stepped up again, so that the high, rare note is recreated. The same principle has been applied to moving pictures—to take through a filter a black and white film which would have all the tones, though not all the tints, of the color spectrum of visible light, and then to run this seemingly only black and white film through a complementary filter, when a colored film would be seen. The principle was tried out to photograph the Delhi Durbar of King George V, but until now synchronization has held it up. The difficulties with sound are not so great, so I overcame them without wasting too much time."

"Well," I had to own, "that is, I must say, peculiarly ingenious. But what happened when the gramophone stopped? You couldn't keep it on till nightfall?"

"I own I was a little uneasy. I kept it going the length of a full record and swept into a sack all the enemy aliens I could. But, apart from requiring them for purposes of research, there was no need. Dr. Cheeseman is right. When an insect's instinctive reaction has been completely thrown out, it cannot, as we do, recollect and carry on. It must go back to its original place, as a man after concussion often has post-lesion amnesia, sometimes of weeks or months or, in a number of well-known cases, of years. So, as they came to, those I hadn't bagged made off and my own broods were free to carry on."

"Did they never come again?"

"Once or twice, but it looks as though some kind of conditioned reflex were being built up in them."

"Well, you'll be free now. I don't know whether you've heard, as we haven't referred to the tragedy, but the coroner told Heregrove to destroy his hives. In the next week or so, at least, I presume the law will see that he has done so."

Mr. Mycroft looked at me.

"I know more of bad men than of bad bees. Heregrove will get rid of the present hives, maybe. But, mark my words, he will not give up beekeeping and the new lot will not be less malignant, but more, if he can make them. A man like that gets the habit, the taste for malicious power. It grows, and it is harder to break than an addiction for morphia. I know."

He evidently spoke with authority, of what sort I couldn't say. I was more anxious to clear up the bee mystery first.

"What is this note which cows them?" I asked.

"Well, as I have said," he replied, "I am sorry not to be able to show you an actual songster. They are harder to come by nowadays than those rare birds in the next room, and far harder to keep. I'll show you, however, a prima donna in her coffin. In fact, here is the form which uttered the voice that routed a thousand murderers and, as you saw a moment ago, can make the most fanatical of all the world's workers down tools and idle as long as her music holds the air."

As he took down a cardboard box which had evidently held note-paper, he added, "Queer, in the bird and animal world, the male sings and the female listens, but in these and some other moths—those, for example, like the purple emperor—with scent we cannot smell—" Suddenly he stopped. "*Am* I getting senile!" he exclaimed. "Would I have overlooked that twenty years ago? Well, this is just like the way a dream is recalled. Suddenly some incident of the day reminds us of a whole dream story which we would otherwise have clean forgotten."

I was completely at a loss as to what he was talking about and waited while he scribbled down a note.

"Forgive me," he said, looking up. "I think showing you this will have helped us more than all the rest of this valuable conversation."

He opened the box. Spread out, fixed with a pin through the fat body, lay a very large moth, curiously marked on the head. "It is the biggest of all the British moths and now quite rare. I had great difficulty in getting a pair. The male is in another box."

"Queerly marked," I said.

"That gives it its name," he replied. "The death's-head moth. But its really odd characteristic is its inaudible voice. It uses that not merely to attract the male but for a purpose as strange as the instrument itself—so as to hypnotize bees, and, when they are so hypnotized, to enter their hives safely and gorge itself on their honey. Fancy holding up a bank only by singing—having to stuff the notes into your mouth all the while, and the bank officials ready to knife you to death the moment your voice gave out! When it comes to the fantastic, we must give the prize to nature every time. We poor creatures who try to imagine the strange are always beaten by the sheer, inexhaustible fantasy of the natural. Well, that shows how I beat off Heregrove's attack and, as I've said, he had no way of telling whether his aerial torpedoes took effect or not. He just guessed that no one else who kept bees would ever suspect that here was a challenge; still less, know how to reply to it."

"And now," I said, firmly, getting up and going to the door, "I am much obliged for a day's most interesting visit. May I have my honey and get home? I presume, now that the sun is sloping and your hives are closing down, none of Heregrove's harpies will be about, even if he has not destroyed them."

"Oh, you are safe enough," he replied. "They won't attack except to protect their hive or to rob another. That is why they came here. That is Heregrove's pretty little game. They root out all other rivals for him. It is really a very neat case of savage instinct being made unconsciously to commit crimes by savage intelligence."

I was nettled by his absorbed interest in his own wretched bees and then in Heregrove's supposed motives. I, obviously, came in only a bad third. Here he had detained me a whole day, under what, it was now clear, were false pretenses. Naturally I had assumed, when he said before lunch that I had better stay, that he said so because it would have been dangerous for me to leave.

"Why," I broke in, "have you then kept me waiting about all day if it would have been quite safe for me to walk home?" I own there was irritation, natural irritation, in my voice.

He showed no surprise or resentment at my rather rough interruption.

"I saw you would not stay simply to hear my explanations," he answered. "You have some of the impatience of a certain Proconsul Pontius who when in a famous, and, as it would seem, important interview, he found the discussion becoming abstract, terminated it with premature irritation, asking what is Truth and waiting not for an answer. So, as you chose to assume that I meant that you were in immediate danger of the bees and would not grasp that your danger really arose from your impatient unwillingness to understand the general character of the peril in which you stand, I permitted your misconception to serve your real interests and kept you here until you had had a fairly thorough demonstration of the factors impinging on your case."

He said this in such peculiarly exasperatingly quiet tones that I need hardly say that his explanation had the reverse effect from soothing my feelings, already on edge. The insult of coolly patronizing me by a lecture on my character was deliberately added to the injury of having used up my whole day. I held my tongue, however, though I felt quite uncomfortably hot. All this explains and shows how natural was my final and, I still think, inevitable protest. He paused. As I have said, I held my tongue with difficulty. And then he went on indifferently, as though there were nothing to apologize for, speaking slowly, as though he hadn't already wasted enough of my time.

"Since showing you that death's-head moth, I think I ought to qualify what I have said. I know how impertinent advice from elders and strangers always seems, and, unfortunately, I am both, but may I request that you do not call on Heregrove without me? I should be very pleased to come with you. Indeed, that was the final point I was going to discuss with you, after which I was not going to detain you any longer."

How could I fail to resent that? I had been treated like a child that has to be tricked to serve its elders' ends, and now, when I was highly and rightly vexed, as if the wasted time were not bad enough, this old dominie was going to force his company still further on me and, in fact, make an attempt to order my life. Who was this old stranger, pushing his advice on me and directing what I should do and whom I should see and in whose care? It was, of course, I felt, quite clear, that he had angled all the time to put me in a position in which I should be unable out of common politeness to refuse his request. He was a clever old crank of a busybody. I hate being managed and maneuvered. Even more, I dislike being made to change my ways and to do precisely the very thing which I live in the country just to avoid doing, taking strangers to call on one's acquaintance. I felt so vexed at this transparent stratagem, coming on the top of everything else—the silly old man with his senile sense of his own tactful finesse, thinking I shouldn't see through it (I was tired too, being kept waiting about all day)—that I felt a positive revulsion against him, and, I suppose by contrast, something almost like clannish protectiveness toward Heregrove.

What was this stranger, gossiper, romancer doing? Making all kinds of insinuations about one of our village—a man about whom I only knew, as a matter of fact, that his honey was always good and quite reasonably priced, and who, poor fellow, had just had his wife killed by his bees which kept me in honey. True, he might not have been very fond of her, but English law had decided, and rightly, that she was the victim of a horrible accident. Even someone you dislike, you can miss very much and be very sorry for, especially if he is suddenly killed in a horrible way. When I was a boy, we had a dog I never really liked. It used to bark and leap up on me—startling and dirtying. Yet when a car dashed over it and there it lay like a smashed bag, I felt not only quite sick, I was really sorry. These thoughts, of course, went in a flash through my mind. I was pretty certainly more tired than I realized.

Mr. Mycroft was standing before me with a rather assured expression on his face.

Before I had thought out the words, I found myself saying: "I'll pay for the honey. I'm a complete recluse and never introduce anyone to anyone else. As to my movements, I have never needed anyone to advise me on them."

I stopped. I own I lacked the courage to meet Mr. Mycroft's eye now that I was being deliberately rude, so I couldn't judge how he took it. All I know is that he passed out of the room without a word. He was away for a few minutes, came back with a neatly made parcel with an ingenious handle made of the string, and named a ridiculously low figure. I fumbled a bit, and I am afraid was a little red as I paid.

All he said was, "The string will hold quite securely. It saves the trouble of a basket being returned."

He held the door open and with a rather clumsy "Good day" I stepped out, hurried across the lawn, now in shadow, into the dusky path through the plantation and so down into the twilit sunken lane. My nerves must have been overstrung (perhaps I had been very discourteous). The whole place seemed unpleasantly still. Those silly, melodramatic lines from *The Ancient Mariner* kept running in my head:

> *Like one that on a lonesome road*
> *Doth walk in fear and dread,*
> *And having once turned round walks on,*
> *And turns no more his head;*
> *Because he knows a frightful fiend*
> *Doth close behind him tread.*

I didn't really feel at all comfortable until I was back in my own sitting room, with the lamp lit, the curtains drawn, and the door well bolted.

4

FLY TO SPIDER

THE NEXT morning, however, I was quite cheerful. Only one thing seemed clear in the gay morning light. By observing my rightful impulse I had—at the cost of a moment's unpleasantness—escaped what might well have turned out to be a permanent invasion by a loquacious, opinionated, fantastic old bore—the very thing, I repeat, that one lives in the country to avoid, the special terror of town clubs and gardens. I was well stocked with honey. I put the whole question out of my head—even of what I would do when my supplies again ran out.

It seemed only a few days, however, before they did. It must, of course, have been a month, perhaps a little more. I remember that I evidently didn't want to notice that I was running low, for it was Alice who drew my attention to it and I was vexed with her. It was really her fault. She should have seen that it was quite clear I did not want to be troubled. But somehow the poorer people are and the stupider, the more they seem to expect you always to be reasonable and clear and sensible.

"You 'ave only 'alf a pot an' one comb now left, sir," was her opening.

"I know," I said, as a silencer. It was as ineffective as my effort to stem the obituaries of the late Mrs. Heregrove.

"An' you 'aven't, sir, rightly even that: the combs run so in this 'ot weather."

I grunted. Human speech of any sort, however astringent, seemed only to act as warm water to a hemorrhage. "An' where you'll be getting your new lot I can't but be wondering. There's never a hive now all round the neighborhood. 'Iveless Hashton, that's what my young man he called it the other day, an' he's right. He's a cure, 'Iveless Hashton."

This was too much, to have the cold and clotted wit of Alice's walker-out served to me after breakfast.

"Alice," I said, with a firmness which I don't remember showing for a very long time, unless it was when I broke away from the tentacles of Mr. Mycroft, "Alice, please get on with your work"—the breakfast table was half cleared, half the china was already marshaled on its transport tray for the kitchen, half still held its position on the table—"and I will get on with mine."

What that was, as I had been looking out the window when the attack had been launched, was not very clear, but I felt I must soften my rebuke by showing that we both had duties which forbade further waste of time. But Alice was wounded. I was being, I could see, not merely rude—that was an employer's right, but "not sensible," and that is something which the rustic mind finds far more upsetting than insult. The wound led to a further hemorrhage of words.

"Well, sir, I was never one to hoffer advice hanywhere, not even in the right quarters" (advice again!), "but I did think it seemed positively silly-like to get yourself with no honey—you being that fond of it and suspicious-like of shop things, as indeed I'm myself; an' all I meant, and no imperence intended and never was, that I'd 'eard that, maybe, you might again be able to be getting yer honey at Heregrove's."

I couldn't help starting a little. Alice was no doubt encouraged by this sign that her attack had made some impression.

"M'young man works up in fields beyond Heregrove's place and 'e's sure 'e's seen Heregrove tending bees as before."

I did want to know more but I was determined even more strongly to check Alice before after-breakfast conversations became established as a precedent.

"Thank you, Alice," I said. "I will look into the matter myself."

I was cold and stiff. I was rude. But I was being

sensible. I was not being "simply whimsey." The stiff-
ness, therefore, did not matter. It might wound, but
the cut was aseptic. Alice was quite content. She had,
of course, not had her talk out, as no doubt she would
have liked, but she had made me do something. That
was even more important. The gentry had been made
to mobilize. I had been compelled to take command.
Off she sailed, contented in her way, and soon the
drone-drawl of "Abide with me" mixed with crockery
clackings came through the baize door—a sure sign
that Alice was enjoying that sentimental sense of having sacrificed herself to make someone else uncom-
fortable, which I believe bitter-sweetens the whole
lives of the industrious poor.

But as I realized Alice's victory I was not so pleased.
I should have to do something. I couldn't and wouldn't
go back to my old bore in Waller's Lane. He, no doubt,
would be glad enough to overlook my unavailing strug-
gle to escape his hold. Alice's victory must not lead to a
rout.

Then there was nothing left to do but to go and
see whether what Alice had said about Heregrove was
true—to spy out the land. And, after all, if he was again
tending bees, there was nothing wrong in that. Of course
he had got rid of the mad hive which had attacked his
poor wife. If no one else could keep bees in the district,
why shouldn't he? No doubt he was skillful—that was

all, "bee-handy." These epidemics—foul-brood, Isle of Wight disease, etc.—were always wiping out hives. I had long ago dismissed old Mycroft's romances. All the demonstrations he gave me could easily, I concluded, have been staged by a clever eccentric. Probably he was the dangerous person to be in touch with—a borderline case. As to Heregrove, it was not my duty to boycott an unfortunate and skillful man. If other people chose to do so—well, it was an ill wind which blew no one any good and I should benefit by being his sole customer.

I went over all these points—small ones, they may seem, and no doubt are. "Why all this fuss," a reader might say, "over buying a few pounds of honey?" I have to own that my mind, far down, was far from easy. If I had not dreaded Mycroft's becoming a bore, an intruder, would I have dismissed all he had told me as mere romance and tried to convince myself that he was cracky? I crushed back the thought, but it was there, and the only way to get rid of it seemed to go and see for myself whether Heregrove was actually again bee-keeping, and, if he were, to replenish my stock. So to escape one unpleasant train of thought—old Mycroft's speculations—I ran right onto the other horn of the dilemma—the very source of all these really rather unnerving suspicions.

When one has made up one's mind to hair-cutting or being fitted by the tailor, I've found it always better to get it over. So that very afternoon I deliberately took my afternoon walk up to Heregrove's end of the village. Luck—no, I have decided to say Destiny—decided that the man should be coming down his garden path at the very moment that I reached his gate. I paused and we came face to face.

"I hear you may again be selling honey" was, I thought, a safe enough opening.

It was not very well received, though. He looked at me with a curiously expressionless face. He certainly was not what fashion papers call prepossessing. Dark, strong, resolute, and intelligent—yes, all these, and cold. Where had I seen a face as cold as that? Of course—old Mycroft's; but there it seemed to me that coldness came from detachment, this from hardness. When I was first taken with Mycroft's look I remembered thinking how quietly cool his face was.

This man's face was somehow not quiet in spite of its coldness. It went through my mind that he was deliberately making his features expressionless, not because he did not care what people thought of him but because he was determined to hide something. That thought led to a still more disquieting one. I felt now sure that he was watching me with much more interest than he intended me to recognize. After a pause, which was becoming quite embarrassing to me, suddenly, like an electric light being switched on behind drawn blinds, the face lit up. I felt a queer, baseless, but quite definite conviction that he had suddenly made up his mind about something.

"I am sorry," he said, in a surprisingly low and accentless voice, "to have hesitated in answering. Since my great sorrow and loss I have been much of a recluse and long silences make for slow responses. Yes, I am again keeping bees." Then, after a pause, "My doctor, when I consulted him, said that after a severe shock the best cure is the hardest—to take up the actual thing most associated with the shock—men who have had a bad fall steeplechasing are told to jump fences as soon as they can again sit in the saddle. Of course, the actual hives have been destroyed, but I have a way with bees and am again thriving with them. I don't quite like to put my notice up again but perhaps I can breed queens and make a little that way." (A queer tremor of suspicion from the back of my mind shook me for a moment.) "But I would be glad to have you again as a customer as my poor wife had. I trust that while I have been out of business" (we were now walking up the path and I was aware his eyes had turned toward me though his head was not turned) "you have not suffered any inconvenience?"

"No," I said, evasively. "No."

I knew I ought to make up some story but, as I've said, living by oneself, one doesn't have to lie and gets out of the habit, at least of doing it convincingly. His next remark showed that I had been right.

"There are, I believe, very few other beekeepers in the district. As homemade honey is so different from the stuff most shops sell, I feared you must have gone without supplies."

I simply said nothing. I could hardly construe that remark as other than a searching question devised to discover where any other beekeepers might be lurking in the locality. However, he must take my silence as he wished. We reached the house and he showed me into the parlor, still as distressing a room as when I had seen it in his wife's day, from my casual glimpses through the door.

I heard his voice behind me continuing, "—Unless, of course, you went far afield hunting your honey?"

The chuckle he gave at this minimal joke did nothing to cheer me. The house, the man, my suspicions, all grated together. I turned around.

"I should like the same supply as I had before," I said.

He named the exact amount and then added, "Come with me. I store near the hives. It saves trouble when in the winter one has to feed them some of their own. Pure sugar is never enough."

Again I felt even more strongly the wish to be out of it all, felt a quite strong resentment toward Mycroft— why could he not have kept from boring me and just

supplied me with honey?—and even a wave of irritation at Alice. Still, to refuse would be ridiculous. We left
the house and went down the back garden path along
which, I remembered, I had seen him, in his wife's time,
going toward the stable.

Because that memory flashed through my mind
and for the sake of saying something not to do with
bees or honey and to break the silence on my part, I
asked, "Do you still keep a horse?"

I own I might have taken such a remark made to
myself by a stranger as impertinent, interfering. But of
course I didn't mean it as that. It was one of those pointless, stopgap remarks we make when we fear a silence
may become too awkward. The remark did have a bad
effect—there was no doubt as to that—a surprisingly bad effect. Heregrove stopped and turned on me. I
looked round and confronted an unpleasantly searching glance. Another of those horrid pauses, and then
the very commonplaceness of the reply only disturbed
me more.

"No, I sold the horse some time ago. I couldn't afford
to keep it."

"That's frank and obvious," I said to myself, but
something in me told me I must have put a finger almost
on the bolt which fastened down some grave secret in
the man's mind. However, the thought that one is alone,
talking to a dangerous fellow who suspects that you may

know too much, is so disturbing that I chose, not unnaturally, the alternative, which had certainly still as good a case—that here was a poor creature who had had very bad luck (or an ill deal from Destiny) and whom I could help by helping myself to his honey. We seldom fear those whom we feel we can patronize. Fear is a beastly feeling, while patronizing always faintly warms one, though we don't like saying so. I needed warming, for I felt more than a slight chill of foreboding, so I changed the subject. The overgrown and bedraggled flower beds caught my eye.

"Even now that most of the best of the summer flowers are over," I prattled, "yet there are enough to keep the bees busy. Queer little creatures." I ran on, as my companion kept silent and I was determined that there should be talk, if only mine and only to reassure myself. "I suppose it's not color but scent which really guides them?"

Again I was aware I was being sidelongly looked over. But how could such babble do anything but reassure a suspicious character? Alas, I knew I was only fooling myself or trying to convince myself that my efforts had done anything of the sort. On the contrary, do what I would, everything I said and even my silences quite obviously heightened his suspicion, and, what was even more disconcerting, made him quite clearly resolved to hold on to me—I supposed to find out whether I was as innocent as I looked or as suspicious as I apparently kept on sounding.

We had reached the end of the garden and the bee-hives were now in view on the other side of a rather dilapidated railing. The hives themselves were in order. When we reached the fence, Here-grove seemed suddenly to change his mind.

"If you will wait here," he said, civilly enough, "I will fetch the honey. It is in that small shed alongside the hives. Most of the bees are already in but, you see, a few latecomers are still coming home. They might be a little irritable. Hard workers on returning home may get cross if they find strangers hanging about their doors."

He smiled as he said this; I was so glad of this sign of improving relations that I tittered rather foolishly in my effort to show my friendliness. He turned his back on me and in a few moments reappeared out of the shed with the load of honey.

"Well, that's done," I thought. "Somehow I shall have to find some other supply, or cure myself of the taste. For I don't think I can face another visit like this." But I spoke to myself before I was out of the wood.

As he came toward me he said coolly, "Before you go, we can just step across to the stable, as we are down at this end of the garden. I'd like to show you the place, as you expressed an interest in the horse I once kept."

The excuse for showing me the place was so palpably

inadequate that I was filled with a queer panic. Yet when I thought of how I could reasonably get out of going the fifty yards he asked me to go and looking into the tumble-down shed, I could see no reason to refuse, as there was obviously no possible peril in going just there, beyond what I might be exposed to in getting straight back to the road. Granted that he had some reason other than he alleged for wanting to show me the place, it was equally clear that that reason could not be to do me any harm. He would hardly wish to injure the first customer of the trade he was trying to revive. I made some sort of assenting sound and turned to follow him as he had already started walking toward the stable. I did this a little more willingly as I was slightly reassured to have him walking in front of me, not I in front of him, and as his hands were full of the jars and combs it was clear he would be a little handicapped if he did intend to assault me.

"Unless, of course," I said jauntily to myself, "he intends to turn on me, pelting me with honey, and so suffocate me. Clarence with his Malmsey; Sydney in his honey."

Joking with oneself sometimes works, but if it doesn't, you are all the worse off. I don't know whether it worked or not then. Perhaps it did, for at least I remember making aloud to Heregrove some little jest about last year's mare's nest when we stood rather pointlessly looking at the wisps of sodden hay that still lined the floor. I think my titter or chuckle did not sound too forced, though Heregrove did not join in. In fact, he seemed hardly to hear me. Where before he had seemed all too vigilant, now he seemed positively absent-minded. When he spoke he seemed almost to be speaking to himself and forgetting me.

"I used to fasten her up in this stall," he said, putting down his armful of honey and going over to the manger.

Out of courtesy I followed. Perhaps, I thought, he was really attached to the horse. Some misanthropes have to find an outlet for their affection. For myself, I don't dislike people—just don't require them—so I suppose I don't have to have pets.

"The little mare," he went on, "could look out of this window. I couldn't give her much exercise, and horses, you know, get bored if kept without anything to do; take to crib-biting and air-swallowing. But she had a nice view here and could look out at things and did, and used to whinny at birds and dogs."

The man was a sentimental recluse suffering from incipient brain-softening, I concluded. I must humor him and get away.

"Just look," he said, straining to see out the stall window, which was high and hard to see out of because of the manger underneath it. "If you look right, you see away to the road; straight ahead, meadows for quite a mile; and down to the extreme left, the road and the tops of the village roofs."

I stretched up to oblige him by looking out. To my relief he moved away.

"The little horse had a fine view, hadn't she?" he asked.

"Yes," I replied. "Yes."

After all, the man was only a fool and could become dangerous only if one insulted the memory of his dear departed mare (who perhaps in some way was, as psychologists say, "surrogate" for his dead wife). I would play the part he wanted me to play and as friends we would part—for good.

"Yes," I said, straining up again and looking all round the view. "There are the woods and the meadows and the village roofs. As pretty an outlook as one could wish."

I turned around; I was alone. Panic took me. I began to rush toward the door. I noticed the honey still on the floor. That would not have checked me. What did check me was to find Heregrove in my path. He must have seen my alarm, but he showed no sign that he did.

"Yes," he remarked, quietly carrying on the conversation, "it's a nice little view."

"Where did you go?" I blurted out.

He looked surprised. "I was only looking in at the other stall. There's room for a couple of horses here. The rats get in that side. I must set a trap there." And then he did something which surprised me and yet queerly reassured me. "I've cut my finger on a nail I didn't see down there when I was lifting a board to see the rat's hole better," he remarked, holding out his right hand. There was a piece of stained rag half wound round his index finger. "I always keep disinfectant about. Apt to get a nasty place if you don't dress it at once when you work in stables and gardens. I can't tie this up, though. Would you be so good just to knot it for me?"

The fact that the man had hurt himself and would put himself in my power placed me again quite at my ease. He might be cracky, pretty certainly was, but he was certainly harmless.

"Gladly," I said. I did feel glad with an almost unreasonable relief.

I am fairly deft with my fingers and wound the bandage neatly, but a lot of the dressing, which he had put on very clumsily, got on my fingers and even on the cuff of my coat. In fact, I suggested taking off the whole bandage because it was clear that owing to his gaucheness he had got more of the disinfectant on the outside of the lint than on the inside. He wouldn't hear of that.

"No, no, it will do finely as it is; don't bother."

"But are you sure," I pressed, "that the dressing has covered the cut? And oughtn't you have washed it out?"

"I did," he replied. "There's a tap in the other stall. The cut was quite small, though deep. And this disinfectant, though it hasn't a nice smell, is quite wonderful with cuts."

Well, he knew his own business best, and my job was to make a good getaway as soon as I could. Certainly the smell of the disinfectant was highly unpleasant; rank was the only word for it. I remembered as a child (smells bring back memories startlingly) being taken to the Zoo and becoming quite nauseated in the small-cat-house. "Small but strong," my father had laughed; but I was retching when I got outside. And the smell of this dressing brought back that memory so strongly that suddenly I thought I should vomit. I hesitated to ask whether I could wash my fingers, but as Heregrove did not make the offer and my own overmastering wish was to get out of the stable, out of the place, out of his company, I started incontinently for the door.

"But your honey," he said.

I had to bear being loaded with the stuff, had to fumble for my purse. But at last we were going down the garden path and I was headed for home and freedom.

As we reached the gate, Heregrove remarked, "I made a poor bundle."

"It's all right," I protested.

"Well, I think I can arrange it a little better in your

hands, so it won't fall before you reach home." And he began to pat the paper and arrange my sleeve and pull out the lapel of my coat, which he said would get crushed.

I simply hate being pawed; and being pawed by a man who, however groundlessly, you mistrust, and who, with every pat, puts a revolting smell under your nose—all that turns an insult into an injury. Literally I broke away from him.

"Thank you," I stuttered, "thank you. Thank you. Quite all right. Will do nicely—splendidly."

I sidled off rapidly with my load, like a small crab which just scuttles under a rock before a gull gets a firm hold on it and pecks it to death. I glanced back in the dusk; the last thing I saw was Heregrove making his way again across to the stables.

I hustled on until I was safe once more in my own place. I had never come back so upset from anything. My return from my upset with Mr. Mycroft was child's play compared with this. Then I had been irritated and a little nervous; now I felt something beside which that had been almost amusing. For a moment I was so spent and foolishly anxious that I felt I would have been positively welcoming if I had heard that assured old voice at the door. It *would* have been reassuring and I needed reassurance.

5

THE FLY IS MISSED

STILL, JUST as after my upsetting visit to Mr. Mycroft, so on this morning succeeding my latest upset, I woke with every care off my mind. "Perhaps when you live very securely by yourself a little upset, even a little fright, is occasionally good for you," I thought to myself as I lay in bed listening to Alice laying the breakfast things downstairs. "It may stir the liver, or the glands, or something which needs a slight emotional rub-down now and then." Certainly the sound of one's comfortable life being got ready again for one to enjoy was particularly pleasant that morning. I bathed leisurely, the more to relish my enjoyment, and also in the hope that, if I dallied, Alice would have, in her argot, slipped up the village and popped in a little 'ouse'old shopping, and so I would be quite secure in the unadulterated pleasure in my own reserved way of life.

My plan worked. When I got down, the house was

all for myself. The kettle simmered on its trivet with a sense of completely reassuring, comfortable patience. The toast was in the grate. I like my toast hard but hot. The eggs were ready to be put in the spirit-stove boiler, which was simmering also with well-bred efficiency. I dropped the eggs in, looking at my wrist watch, and brought the toast onto the table. Took from the hob the warmed teapot—brown earthenware—I keep my Georgian silver for afternoon tea—gave it the three spoonsful of Lap-sang and poured the boiling water neatly onto the leaves.

It was, as it happens, the fragrant smoky smell, faintly tarry, but very refined, which brought back that abominable disinfectant of Heregrove's into my thoughts. I was (I always am) in my dressing gown at breakfast. I remembered now that on coming in I had put my jacket in the wardrobe, meaning to have it sent to the cleaners. I had carefully washed my hands, but I could, when I looked closely, still see a slight discoloration on the sides of my two fingers, and when I raised them to my nose I could yet detect very faintly, but still unmistakably, that smell. But you had to put your nostrils quite near to get it. I thought, though, I would see what another scouring would do. Landing the eggs, I ran up the stairs. After a rapid scrub, which I had to own did not diminish much that last, queer, clinging taint, I decided I must keep my head up and it must and would wear off. Passing through the bedroom, however, I thought that I had better see how the jacket itself had fared. I took it out of the wardrobe, with some apprehension, but there, too, the smell seemed mainly to have evaporated. It did smell, of course, if you put your nose right on it, but you wouldn't notice it a few inches away. As I'm very forgetful about dull routine details such as laundering, I took the jacket down with me and placed it on a chair beside the table.

"That will remind me," I thought, "to tell Alice, when she comes back, to have it cleaned."

Then I again marshaled the table, but a moment later I was again on my feet. Alice had put out for me that last running comb, about which she had spoken—as a mute reminder, I supposed, should I have failed to act. Her observations had been correct: nearly all the honey had gone out of it and, as she had neatly changed the plate, I was left with practically nothing but solid wax to eat. I am economical, but wax is not very pleasant or good for you. I had my new supplies, won with considerable discomfort. A few steps into the larder and there they were—neatly unpacked and stacked, each covered with a pyrex baking dish on white plates ranged along the slate shelf. I lifted one of these and brought a fine, sound comb with me to the breakfast table.

The windows were open, for though the day was not yet hot, it was clear and fine and the fire kept my feet warm. I was munching away in that quiet unthinking state of mind which is perhaps the nicest thing about meals by oneself, when one becomes like a placid animal chewing the cud under a tree in summer, so much at my ease that I was really not thinking of anything in particular. Everything seemed generally all right. So I can't say when I first became aware that this was no longer quite so.

Our hearing is said to be our most vigilant, unsleeping sense—last to go when we lose consciousness and first to come back when we regain it, even before we know where we are. I think it was hearing something without attending to it which gave me my first sense of undefined uneasiness. Humming sounds are generally reassuring, but this, for some reason, wasn't. Then a couple of bees flew in at the window. I thought at first they were wasps (though we have had few this year) after my honey. I held my knife ready to knock out the robbers directly they should alight. They zoomed above the honey but did not alight on it, and then suddenly swooped on the coat hanging on the chair. They settled on the sleeve and lapel, and at that moment the hum broke into full cry, as though a pack had viewed their fox. I saw a dense swarm of bees sweep down outside, wheel before the window, and come pouring into the room. They rushed, without a moment's check, to join the few scouts already settled on the coat. In a moment it was black with them. I started back, for I could see they were not investigating. They weren't even crawling about. Each was convulsively clinging to the worsted: they were stinging and restinging the cloth, piercing it through with their deadly little sabers.

Fortunately, the staircase was near me, and the chair with the coat on it at the other side of the table, or this story would have been written, if at all, by another hand. I scrambled toward my escape. My movement, however, must have given some alarm to the swarm, for quite a large group detached itself from the coat and swung into the air to investigate me.

I thought I could still manage safely to beat my retreat, when one bee, swinging past me, went within a few inches of my hand. Like a shot he threw himself on it. I knocked him off, trod on him, and threw myself up the stairs, flinging my dressing gown over my head to shield, if possible, my face and neck. This desperate stroke evidently made such a whirlwind in the small staircase that it momentarily drove down my flying attackers; but I saw, as I turned, that the whole swarm had now left the coat and were wheeling round to fling themselves after me.

A moment's wild scramble and I was through the bedroom, dashing over the furniture, had gained the bathroom and slammed the door. Rushing to the window, I slammed that down. Outside the door I heard the angry buzz and even the sinister little taps of the bees flinging themselves in murderous frenzy on the panels. A moment later I saw a couple come crawling from under the door. I stamped on them and felt an unpleasant glee as their bodies crunched on the tile floor. They were deadly as flying snakes, but my heel could still bruise their heads once they were forced to crawl.

I had begun to feel (very unreasonably, considering my actual situation) something of the thrill of victory, when, suddenly, a sensation like a mixture of an electric shock and a severe scald shot along my leg. Tearing up my pajama trouser, I saw a bee, its sting thrust into my shin a few inches above the ankle. I struck it down and crushed it and wedged a towel along the threshold crack of the door. I must have carried the brute with me into the bathroom. I remember looking over myself to see if there were any others, and then looking back at the sting, which had already swollen into a large black lump like a rotten chestnut. Then the pain, which had been rising like a tide, became so intense that I must have fainted.

The next thing I saw was that the door was open and the lock forced. That vexed me.

"The jamb is broken," I began, petulantly. "Who did that?"

I was addressing myself to someone I sensed was near me. Then I realized how odd it was to be talking lying on the bathroom floor, whether the lock had been smashed or no. I remembered everything in a flash.

"Shut the door!" I cried.

"It's all right," said a deliberately soothing voice. I was just going to try to get up when the speaker bent over me. "Don't move, just for a moment," he advised. "We've put a towel under your head. I'd just like to listen to your heart and have a look at that place on your leg before you get up."

It was young Jones, who, I had heard, was the new village junior medico—a smart young junior to help elderly Dr. Abel. Quite a bright fellow, I'd heard people at the post office remarking. He had his stethoscope sounding me in a moment, remarking, as he listened, "Um, all right now." Then to me, "Sorry to be so professional as well as intruding. Truth is, when your maid suddenly haled me in I thought at first sight she was right and you were in for something ugly."

I caught sight of Alice's face; she was standing in the bedroom wearing that expression of mingled woe and triumph, distraction and self-importance, which is the proper guise of those who have the distinction of having a tragedy in their house. That both amused and reassured me. I still felt a lot of pain as well as numbness in the leg; it was burning as though being scorched before a fire and throbbing as though it would burst. But I was apparently safe, for there was no menacing buzz to be heard and my two attendants seemed wholly concerned for me and unaware of any possibility of peril to themselves.

"How did you manage to wound yourself like that when you fell?" Dr. Jones asked, turning round from examining my shin.

"How did I manage!" I exclaimed. "Look at those dead bees on the floor! I was attacked when at breakfast by a swarm and only got in here just in time. That, thank heaven, is the one sting I suffered. Half a dozen and your help would have come too late."

"Attacked by a swarm coming into the house and going for you?" he replied, with obvious incredulity. "Besides, I have never seen anyone react in that way to bee venom. You must be highly allergic to such irritations."

"Highly allergic to irritation!" I shot back. "Those bees were no normal bees. Those bees were sent—"

Dr. Jones turned to Alice and said, in the sort of aside voice which doctors use when they are getting a second opinion on a patient's statement, "Did you see any bees when you came in?"

"Well, sir, now you comes to ask me, p'r'aps there was a few about, as you might say, or maybe they was wapses, for we've hardly a waps till now, and of course we ought to be having 'em all along with the plums and such—"

"But you didn't see a swarm of bees?"

"I was just a-coming through the gate with me 'ands full up with parcels, for I'd slipped up to the village to pop in a little shopping before the shops get too full with the quality to get things quickly. As I say, perhaps there was a bit o' buzzing about, but what give me the turn was as soon as I'd put foot in the 'ouse to see the tablecloth all pulled awry, toast an' honey and egg on the carpet, napkin on the stairs, bedroom chair flung over and bathroom door shut 'n' locked, an' the 'ouse still as a death. My grandpa died of a fit just that way. Just flew off, you might say. So I rushed out to get 'elp and there by 'eaving's mercy were you a-going by."

It was clear that, however long Alice talked, this would be the substance, the sole substance of it. Dr. Jones would list me as a prize allergic, thrown into a seizure by a single bee sting, which any normal person would take with as little fuss as stubbing his toe against a table. Well, perhaps it was best. The bees, baffled for a moment, and losing close track of their prey, had evidently veered off as swiftly as a line-squall. And even if my story were told, who would believe it?

"You had better keep that leg up today, and, if you like, I'll take a look at it this evening. You certainly are intensely allergic" (there came that irritating, glozing phrase) "to bees. You should keep out of their way. Must say you seem to have chosen a spot where you can do that. Except for these few, that you say came on a special visit to you, I don't know when I last saw bees about here, except a few down Waller's Lane. Perhaps they were cross because they were lonely, or perhaps people who are highly allergic attract their allergy, if it's a living creature."

These speculations, evidently intended as pleasantries, did not amuse me. Obviously these bees could be no joking matter for me; on the contrary, they were nothing less than a matter of life and death. I was quite ready to keep indoors until I could think what to do, and the excuse of my stung leg was one small good out of what otherwise looked a wholly bad business. Dr. Jones and Alice helped me to the sofa which stands beside my south bedroom window. I thanked him and asked him not to trouble to call again unless I sent him a message. When he was gone and Alice was back, viewing me with a proprietary eye, I was able to effect another small stratagem.

"I feel chilly," I said. "Please close all the windows and keep the door shut."

"And I don't wonder you do feel a chill," she agreed. "Why, when my pore, dear grandpa was taken with the fit that put him off, 'e went as cole as a stone. You'd 'a' 'ardly thought it was flesh, so cold and clammy-like. Cold flesh to cold earth, I can just hear my ma saying, and she was right."

"Alice," I struck in, "my head is aching a little. Please go downstairs and make me a little tea and some toast."

"Mercy me, and you with no breakfast, all the time you've been lying here and lying there, as you might say."

"Alice, I need the tea now," I remarked, with all my weight on the ultimate word.

Alice was gone. Respect for command and pity for the wounded state acted as a double charge.

I was left to my thoughts. They could hardly be cheerful. Here was a desperately cunning man who, starting perhaps with some slight suspicion of me, now evidently for sport, if for no other reason, was set on killing me and in an abominably agonizing way, just to show off his malicious power and to experiment with an instrument of death, which, when perfected, he could employ with absolute precision and equal impunity. He had just missed, but only by bad luck (or Destiny). But the second shot would probably succeed; and there was no one who would believe my story or who, even if they believed, so long as they hesitated to act on it, arrest the man and destroy his diabolical bees, could give me any protection. I must skulk in the house, till the cold weather put my fiendish persecutors to sleep, dreading all through the summer every hum of a blow-fly—a miserable creature forced to hibernate all the warm weather and only able to go abroad and have any freedom and happiness of the slightest sort so long as the weather was raw and cold.

I heard Alice's step on the stairs. As I could not face more reminiscences of her ancestors' ends and the similarity of their fates to mine, I pretended to be dozing. I heard her come in, shut the door, and place the tray beside me, but after doing that she did not leave the room. I opened an eye warily and found her regarding me in a dubious way.

"Sorry, sir, to disturb you, and you 'aving 'ad such a morning. But downstairs, asking, as he can't remember, whether, 'as used to 'appen, he lent you a basket—you ain't a-going to faint again!"

My head was whirling.

"Alice," I said, in what I fear was only what novelists call a hoarse whisper, for I had no control of my voice, "Alice, go down at once and get that man out of the house. You know I never allow visitors. And see," I almost gasped, "he doesn't take anything with him."

Alice was electrified.

"'Im a common thief! Well, I'd not put it pass 'im."

She whisked out of the room, closing the door quickly behind her. I strained my ears, heard some short sentences, and then her foot was again upon the stair. I positively welcomed it.

"'E's gone, sir," she said. "I was too quick for 'im. All I said was, 'Master's lying up. I look after the 'ouse. There's no basket of yourn here,' and with that I shut the door'n him and watched 'im through the winder go off down the path."

I lay uneasily all day upstairs. After she had served me my lunch, I told Alice to go back to her parents' house, where she lives.

"You can call in again about five," I said.

She went off gladly, no doubt looking forward to retailing all the details of my accident and both noting and hearing how well it agreed with a number of fatal precedents.

As soon as she was well out of the house and I had seen her hat bob its course above the hedge on its way to the village, I hobbled off the sofa and scrambled down the stairs. The room had been tidied, but my jacket was still lying on the chair and the chair was standing by the door of the living room which opened into the hall. Anyone waiting at the front door would see the chair with the jacket on it. A couple of quiet steps, while whoever answered the door was away on some bogus message—I snatched up the jacket. It fell from my hands. I remembered quite clearly that when I took it down there had been a handkerchief in the breast pocket. It was gone.

The door was locked, thank heaven. Not that my tormentor was likely to attack me with any instrument but the secret, horrible, agonizing one he had forged— and a taste of which was making my whole leg at that moment throb and burn. But the locked door gave me a little comfort, in knowing that I was screened from any chance of his looking at me or walking in on me to gloat on his helpless victim. If I had seen that cold face regarding me I think I might have gone out of my mind.

I dragged myself heavily upstairs. It was all too clear. The monster had come along, cool in his assurance that no one could suspect him, just to see how his bolt had fared; expecting, hoping that he would have found me a bloated, purple corpse. Finding, however, that his first cast had failed to kill, he had quietly walked in and taken something which would have my scent. It was obvious, he was hard at working out some new plan whereby—as he could scarcely hope to inveigle me within his pawing range a second time—he might manage to get his hell hornets on my track again by giving them my scent.

Alice came back, gave me my tea, my light early dinner (God save me from nightmares; I had now enough raw material, God knew), and then, after "making me comfortable for the night," as she put it (but which was a task beyond her, or anyone in the village, to effect), she went off. I didn't sleep much.

But why not send for Mr. Mycroft? Of course I thought of it again and again. But in a matter of life and death, such as this had suddenly become, might not any interference make it worse—only precipitate things? Could the old man really protect me with his gadgets? Wasn't the only safe thing to get right out of the village—go clean away—vanish quietly without telling anyone, leaving no address; just tell Alice one was called away on urgent business and then not come back?

Heregrove, I felt sure (it was, somehow, an additionally horrible thought) was killing me out of no particular spite, but just for fun, just because I happened, poor insect, to alight near him when he was trying out a new insecticide. "As flies to wanton boys are we to the gods; They kill us for their sport." It was not a comforting line to dwell on. Yet, I suppose, this kind of thing always does happen when men get the gods' power to kill with absolute impunity. But why should it have happened to me? Why should I be driven out of my house, and even then not be safe? This fiend, for all I knew, might enjoy hunting me with his demonic pack, all over England. Every beast of prey is additionally excited when it sees its quarry break into flight.

It was that thought that decided me. As the light came, I went to my desk and wrote a very apologetic, very humble note. When Alice came I gave it to her as she brought me up my breakfast, for my leg was still as stiff as a staff.

"Down Waller's Lane," she said, looking at the envelope. "Wait for a hanswer. I'd like to do that. They say that Mr. Mycroft's a perfect cure. Keeps himself to himself as others do and 'ave a right to. But he's an inventor person, they say. For 'is cook—"

"I want an answer as soon as possible," I said.

"Very well, sir. I could get down and back while you was getting through your breakfast."

I thanked her and watched her start on an errand which, obviously interesting as it was to her, was of far more moment to me.

6

FLY MADE TO INTRODUCE
WASP TO SPIDER

INDEED, I waited so uneasily that I only toyed with my breakfast. I saw that I was completely thrown out. The even tenor of my life, which I had arranged so carefully, was thrown into complete confusion. There was no honey on the table—that alone was enough to upset me and to remind me how completely my life had been invaded and over-set. But of course it would have been madness to have brought the deadly stuff out into the air to betray me to my enemies. I felt sick at the very thought of my favorite food. That, I reflected, bitterly, is some measure of my misery.

I would have had the whole batch buried, only I wondered whether, while that was being done, it wouldn't attract those fiends. Besides, Alice might think I was going mad. She had remarked how stuffy the house was, with all the windows close shut, and indeed it did seem rather odd on a lovely morning to be keeping everything closed up as though we were already in the middle of winter—winter which, though I usually dislike the season, I had now begun positively to desire. And already she and the doctor she had foolishly called in were now secretly agreed that I was cracky and liable to fits and "uniquely allergic" and fanciful and subject to frantic illusions and God knows what else. It would need only another couple of false steps, which in my strung-up condition I might all too easily take, and there would be dolorously delighted, hysterical Alice and sharp master medico Jones together (and, of course, with the noblest intentions) landing me in the asylum!

I could hear Alice tearfully but triumphantly indicating to the two magistrates who would commit me, how much my case resembled not only her grandfather's but also that queer old aunt's, who first thought she was being eaten by cockroaches and then that all her family were cockroaches and so tried to extirpate the gargantuan pests by throwing quicklime in their faces. She would add no end of confirmatory details—my queer, secretive ways, my morbid distaste for talk, my little rules for having my things just so and for not being intruded on. I could see Dr. Jones nodding his head approvingly; giving some silly, impressive Greek name to every bit of behavior which Alice retailed. I was, of course, an acute case of agoraphobia, in an advanced condition of schizophrenia. That taste for honey? Oh, that was conclusive—oncoming G.P.I. They always have a morbid appetite for carbohydrates, especially for the sugars. No safer symptom. A typical paresia-seizure in the bathroom. A spinal puncture must be made at once. A stiff dose of one of the arsenical compounds—dangerous, of course, but might save us (not *me*, please note) from worse things. The patient (of course I had already lost any personality, let alone rights) ought to be put under the heat treatment without delay. Keep him at a temperature of 105° for some time and his sanity might return. No, he couldn't take any responsibility if the patient was left at large.

I saw myself made the most awful of convicts in a moment by these four well-meaning nincompoops. I saw myself taken off in a closed car, holding onto my self-control, knowing I was being watched as a certified madman and every move or remark I made being immediately interpreted as confirming my lunacy. I saw us arrive at that abominably misnamed place, the asylum, no refuge but the one place the sane must dread with an almost insane terror. I saw myself taken in charge, I who had always resented and avoided and lived to escape the slightest control or authority or being managed. I saw myself holding on ever more tremblingly to my last shreds of independence and self-mastery. I saw the quiet, convincing conviction in every face round me that I was mad and was only an incurably deranged machine dumped in this junk-house of broken minds. I saw myself making my last stand, saying to myself, "Well, they shall not have a shred of excuse for thinking I'm in the slightest way different from any of their stupid selves, too stupid to be mad!"

And then I saw, into the hard, white, prison-like room, through the hygienically wide-open window, right toward us, swoop one of those diabolical bees. I saw myself involuntarily duck and call out to them to take cover. I saw them (as in a nightmare but, oh, so inevitably) pay no attention to my actual words or to the bee. Even if one of the damned fools *were* stung, the rest of them would be so delighted at this beautiful little demonstration of my specific madness that they would have no attention for anything but my "seizure." I could hear them, in that clipped, conclusive, colloquial, group-assuring jargon, confirming one another's idiocy, "Typical case." "Trigger action." "Frenzy brought on by associative symbol."—Symbol! I could only hope that the stung medico was stung in some quite unsymbolic part—not that his pain would disturb their stupid equanimity and blind assurance. "Perfect example of hymenophobia." "Must study this for a clinical paper; a valuable demonstration. Old Singleton will be fascinated with such a complete case." And all the while they would be scurrying me along those long, high-lit passages; I, held in one of those oh-so-gentle-but-move-a-finger-and-your-wrist-will-break jiu-jitsu grips, and they talking of the bundle in their hands, of me, as though I were a corpse being lugged along to its autopsy!

I had just reached that pleasant climax of my all too convincing extrapolation of the remainder of my days; I was just imagining, with complete realization, night and day succeeding one another without feature or finitude, until I really fell in with their idea of me, until I was so persuaded by my unchanging situation that they must be right and I wrong that I would actually demonstrate for them. I would be brought into the lecture theater of the mental hospital and sit there amiably huddled in the demonstration chair, while students and their friends looked at the interesting specimen, the queer animal, and the lecturer told its history and indicated its peculiar points of interest, finally letting fly a bumblebee in my face. I would then obligingly go off into my seizure and be carted out by the attendants. But, just as they pounced on me, I saw, sitting high up in the visitors' part of the theater, looking down on me with a delight in this torture worse than death by poison, the face of Heregrove!

I had just arrived at such a pretty peep into the hell that seemed now all too likely to lie ahead, when I heard not one set but two sets of footsteps on the gar-

den path. Though I was well screened, for I always curtain my windows heavily—in my opinion, houses were
not meant to be glass hives, as some modern architects
seem to think—and though the path from gate to front
door went round to the other side of the house (I always
have my bedroom in the quietest place), I was so nervous now that I drew back and positively cowered in
my chair. The front door opened and I heard muttered
voices. I knew it was highly improbable, but somehow
reason was no help and emotion only said with every
pound of my heart: "They've *come* for you! They've
come for *you!*"

Then there was a step on the stairs. I picked up a
piece of cold, brittle toast. I must appear to be eating
unconcernedly; I must make a last fight for my sanity
and for being thought normal. I was hardly given time
to answer the knock, and my throat was so dry I probably couldn't have said clearly "Come in."

"Why, and you've not even finished your breakfast
now, and me gone ever so!"

It was very impertinent of Alice to make such a
personal remark, but I was shattered by all that I had
been through and foreseen. I felt so strongly that her
very "imperence" was a sort of semiconscious suggestion that she thought I was already half-certifiable and
an intuitive test to see whether I would break out, that I
answered in a positively demure, sub-acid voice, steady

and quiet, though it shook a little to my feeling if not to her ear.

"Who has accompanied you into the house?" I felt that, though such a question to Dr. Jones would sound rank with agoraphobia and blatant with schizophrenia, to Alice it would be the best approach. She was still mainly my servant and I, at least for a few days more and as long as I was let be at large, her employer. Thank God, she reacted according to her type.

"Oh, please, sir, I was only sorry to see you'd not fancied your breakfast. No imperence was meant, sir. I 'ope I'd never forget m'place. And as for bringing in someone—well, sir, I couldn't 'elp myself. He's so quick and direct, is—" (I could not but feel my heart pounding even harder) "is Mr. Mycroft."

Somehow, at the mention of that name, my heart suddenly was free. It positively leapt. Bore or no bore, would not I have the old fellow every day, all my life, if only I need not be shut up. And now I felt certain he was the one man who would understand and could save me from one or the other of two frightful fates which I felt closing in on me.

"Please, Alice," I said, reprovingly, "don't keep Mr. Mycroft waiting downstairs. Go at once. Give him the paper. Offer him some tea. I suppose he has breakfasted. Say how pleased I am that he has called round. Tell him I will be down in a moment."

She went. I hurried with my dressing. I don't have to shave every day, unless I am peculiarly particular. It is more of a massage than a mow. So I was following Alice down the stairs in a very few minutes. Mr. Mycroft was standing by the fireplace as I entered. I must say he put me beautifully at my ease, and I needed it, I need hardly say.

"I have been away, Mr. Silchester," he began, quite easily and naturally keeping the talk away from me; "I have been over to Hungerford—still a nice, small town, with beautiful open country round it. I went for a few walks when I was there. You don't know it? And perhaps you do not care much for walking? I find I enjoy it very much, but, perhaps because I've always been rather a collector-hunter type of man, I find, to enjoy myself really, I have to make some little objective for myself, some small sight to see."

There he was talking about himself, but somehow today it was positively a relief. All too soon we should have to come to my case and, as long as he was here, I felt safe. I felt that I ought to make some slight comment.

"Didn't that amusing writer Lytton Strachey live down there?"

"Yes; in fact, I passed his house, in taking my longest walk. But I wasn't on a literary pilgrimage. His house lies in the vale just before you reach the finest walking in England, the North Downs escarpment. I was bound for that. Right opposite that house's windows stands Inkpen Beacon. I walked there; really after I had done my little piece of hunting, just out of romantic interest." Looking away from me, Mr. Mycroft added, "There used to be a gallows on that crest. The last man hanged on it was a remarkable murderer. Indeed, I should have thought, at that date, more than a century ago, he would have got off. But they brought the charge fully home to him. I was reading up the crime at Hungerford. He was a small Hungerford farmer, living not far from Lytton Strachey's house." Then, turning to me, Mr. Mycroft said, quietly, "He murdered his wife with a simple ingenuity which I have myself not met with elsewhere in the records of homicidal crime: by upsetting her into a hive of angry bees."

I felt myself pale.

"But," he went on, "even at that date, he was caught. And, though time adds to all skill, even in devilry, it also adds to our defenses."

He paused. Then I summoned up my courage.

"Mr. Mycroft, it was extremely kind of you to come round so promptly. I don't expect to be able to conceal from you the condition I am in, a condition to which—"

"Yes," he said, with comforting confirmation. "I have seen plenty of men, who felt they were brave and tough, begin to go to pieces under the strain you have been enduring."

That kindness—what I would call the right professional or medical attitude (I felt now pretty sure the old fellow had been a doctor)—that steady understanding, certainly hit me pretty hard. He took the hand—rather trembling, I fear it was—which I put out and held it in a remarkably reassuring grip.

"You have been doing a useful and dangerous piece of work," he said—a curiously clever way of comforting someone who felt he had been only a bungling, impertinent fool, who had insisted, even when warned, on sticking his silly head all too literally into a hornets' nest, and now was frightened almost out of his wits.

"You have drawn Heregrove," he continued. "As we agreed" (that again was kind; it had, of course, been solely his diagnosis), "Heregrove is the typical murderer-with-a-bright-idea."

I shuddered at the word, but it was true enough.

"That type generally reads a great many detective stories and, as you are no doubt aware, detective stories, like many other of our modes and manners—if you will forgive what may sound like an old man's 'grouse'— have degenerated. They began with common sense and trained observation and perhaps a patient devotion to and belief in tidying things up, these three allied together—not necessarily to exact the law's penalty but to show the criminal he could not win; that the balance of intelligence and insight are, in the end, always on the side of order and right."

The old man was started, but again I felt only relief. I

thought of a long, plodding relief column, pertinaciously winding its way through narrow passes to raise the siege of a sorely beleaguered garrison.

"But now," he went on, "it is the gentleman cracksman who is the public's real fancy. Oh, I know the films have to show the G-man getting his gunman, but that is only a 'command performance.' The public has to see such pictures because it supposes they protect it from young, growing criminals. But the public really likes fancying itself in immaculate evening dress carelessly holding up the bank at Monte Carlo. Well, a few act on their daydreams. They get a new idea, as they think. I have shown you that this one is not as new as our friend believes. They suffer from an old irritation—as old as the world, the returning to 'a dark house and a detested wife'—reverse the roles and the story is certainly as old as cyclopean Mykenae and the Trojan War, Klytemnestra killing her Agamemnon in his bath—older, if we only knew. They kill, and then, like most animals with the instinct to kill in their blood, having tasted blood, they must go on killing. Nothing else gives them such a sense of power—and this feeling they must have. All the members of the human race—proud, successful, hateful creatures—are in the murderer's hand. To them he may seem a failure. They had better beware! At his slightest whim, there they are—so much carrion."

It was all too obviously exemplified by my situation—the casual, nearest-to-hand neighbor following the hated wife into the oubliette.

"What are we to do?" I ventured to interpose.

"Mr. Silchester," he said, looking straight at me, "I am going to repeat a request."

"You needn't have any fear," I interrupted: "I shall never go near the place again."

"The request I made," he went on quietly, "had two clauses. The first, that you should not go alone, has proved to have been wise. The second—" He saw I had gone white. I now remembered it all too well. But he went on serenely, "Was that you would introduce me to your acquaintance, Mr. Heregrove."

"But I can't! It would be suicide for us both. The very sight of the man would make me tremble and he would be bound to make his brutes attack us, even if they did not do so of themselves. Can't you put all you know before the police? Can't you have him arrested?"

"British law is a noble pile," he replied ruminatively, "but, like most stately causeways, erected block by block, year after year for centuries, it has plenty of crannies in it. The liberty of the subject requires that the law should not look too closely. For life and law are never very easy with each other and we must pay for our freedom to be eccentric by letting an occasional criminal get through and away." Then, with a sudden sharpness, "There's not a shred of evidence to go to a court upon. He's proved innocent of his wife's death. A court has said it was an accident. As for your situation: you were attacked in your house and no one even saw it happen. Your servant is hardly a mute. She does not ask to be questioned before she gives you both news and views. She sympathizes sincerely with you for having had some sort of shock. In her family, I gather, similar things have befallen. But she is certainly skeptical about the cause being other than, as she put it, 'in the family.' Indeed, Heregrove might turn the tables on you—he is certainly bold enough to do it—and say you were maligning him; trying to ruin him; either a blackmailer or a border-line neurotic. Remember, Mr. Silchester, an eccentric has few friends."

That so chimed with my own gloomy thoughts at which his visit had found me that I collapsed into a wholly apprehensive silence.

"But remember also," he went on, deliberately cheering, "Heregrove is also curiously helpless, curiously localized in his malignancy. He is like one of those slow-moving, stiff, poisonous lizards which, if you pounce and pick them up in a certain way, can't get their venom-spine into you."

He saw that I remained dolefully unconvinced. So he added, "Believe me, there is no safer place for you than in Heregrove's house. He's playing a game. He's perfecting his lovely, power-giving murder tool. He's not going to spoil all by striking at you when the corpse would fall on his hands."

I didn't like the phrase at all, but it did make the situation clear, if painfully so.

"No, no; in his house you will be under his guard. Some spiders don't recognize a fly if it is not in their web. Heregrove simply can't kill you unless you are outside his."

Still, I quite naturally hesitated. Mr. Mycroft looked keenly at me again.

"And unless we do get into that house we shall never get him off your track. I beg you to make no mistake over that. I have more knowledge of this particular psychology than, if I may say so, you are likely to have. At the proper range, with his perfect shot, he is as determined yet to get you, as a golfer who won't go on to the third green until he has holed out on the second. You are No. 2 on his score."

I knew all too well he was right.

"I must tell you," I agreed, "Heregrove came here, called here, the very day he tried to murder me, only a couple of hours after the attempt!"

"Yes, your Alice told me of what she, though ignorant of the fullness of his nerve, called his 'imperence.' She evidently has something of an animal's intuitive mistrust of malignancy, though she thinks your actual attack was a subjective experience: an interesting case, showing where intuition is sound but helpless, because reason is too rudimentary to argue accurately and attention too bird-witted rightly to observe."

"But, Mr. Mycroft, she could not have told you the worst. When I went downstairs, after he had gone, I discovered that, while he had sent her upstairs on a fake message to me, he had taken the handkerchief out of my jacket pocket, which was lying in sight of the door! Do you see?"

"You needn't explain," he interrupted. "I know I seem to you long-winded, but I won't waste your time on unnecessary details if I can help it, in this case. Time matters here. I'll tell you: the purloining of your handkerchief does not, I think, matter immediately by adding any instant additional peril to that in which you already stand. We have time there. Nor need you explain to me about your coat. When in one of my thinkings aloud, which grated on you so much at our first meeting, I suddenly called myself senile, or at least questioned myself as to whether I might not be becoming so, it was because I had not foreseen that move of Heregrove's. You remember?"

"Yes, we were talking about insects being able to hear sounds that we cannot and how a number of insects track great distances also by smell."

"Well, that was why I begged you not to go to

Heregrove's place alone. I was sure he would want you to come, and I was equally sure, if he could get you by yourself, he would try to put some mark on you whereby his bees could track you down. You played into his hands perfectly. Now, will you tell me exactly what he did?"

I gave Mr. Mycroft precisely the account which I have put down before. I saw his face light up.

"Fascinating," was his first and, I thought, rather heartless comment. He saw that my feelings were hurt and added at once, "I repeat, you did all of us an invaluable service by going there and taking the risk—making Heregrove show his hand before he was perfectly prepared. I believe you made the gun go off half-cock or half-charged. He wasn't quite ready, or he would have found some way of asking you up. But he could not resist when, as he thought (all murderers of that sort are megalomaniacs), Destiny had put you deliberately in his hands. He will know more of Destiny before he has finished. Meanwhile, we must not let our counter-preparations suffer from the same fault. You see now, we *must* call on him. The coat trick failed. As a precaution, have that jacket burned. Tonight put it well into the center of your weed-and-grass bonfire which I saw smoking at your garden's end. At night, mind you. Some virulent essential oils, like that of the pestilential poison oak of the southwestern United States, actually become more pungent and irritating when burning, and that would simply mean that you were signaling to your vampires, asking them to come over and attack you again. Now for your hand."

I showed him the fingers which had been stained. No trace remained which even my nose could detect after all my scrubbings. But he insisted on getting some medical alcohol and rubbing the skin till it was sore.

"Now for something to throw off the scent, or rather to bury it under a load it couldn't pierce through," he remarked, drawing a small bottle from his pocket. "I brought this little mixture with me because I thought Heregrove would have tried some way of 'putting the doom on you,' as our ancestors would have phrased it, and quite accurately, too. I have noticed it throws out any animal's olfactory sense more completely than any one scent. It is citronella, valerian, and aniseed oils in equal parts."

Rubbing it on my fingers, which were almost inflamed by the alcohol, he added, "Now, please go up and wash. We don't want Heregrove to smell us, or he is quite shrewd enough to 'smell our rat.' We only want to be sure to put his bees off. They will certainly smell the anointing I have given you and be of the opinion that you are not the man they wanted so furiously, so little time ago, to kill. The voice may be the voice of Jacob but the smell will be the smell of Esau."

Quotations again; how the old man's mind ran on! I didn't want to attend to his sallies. My mind was in a most unpleasant whirl. It was all too obvious that he was pushing me, caparisoning me, I might almost say, as his mount, to go at once into action, to call straightway on Heregrove.

"I say," I began lamely, hoping, perhaps only to gain time.

He saw my tendency and was quite clear and quick.

"Yes, we must go at once. He must not gain a moment's more time, if we can help it. The fact that you come back again will be, to his cocksure vanity, final proof that you have not been able to put two and two together and so don't suspect in the least his designs. Even should you mention being attacked, he will show you a wondering sympathy, talk of the mysteries of instinct, of how, unless he's with someone they dislike, he's always safe with the bees—they are his friends, like his dear little mare (which, incidentally, he poisoned), and how he can sympathize, having lost his dear wife in the same strange way. The fact that you bring round an amiable if boring old gentleman, also anxious to purchase honey, will put the final seal on your ignorance. You hardly introduce fresh customers to a salesman who you know has just tried to shanghai you."

"All right," I said resignedly.

Only the feeling that I had no choice but to decide

to go back to that den or to be driven out of my house and perhaps out of my mind or out of my body—only such a grim, clear decision made me agree to act. But even then, when I assented, that was not enough for my strange champion.

"No," he said, turning his head on one side and looking at me. "You must play your part a trifle more convincingly than that. As it is, you look as though *you* were the man with the noose closing round his throat. In spite of all Heregrove's insane self-assurance, that look of yours would raise doubts in his mind, and if he doubts, we are done."

I tried to smile, but it was a pale smirk of a thing.

"I'm sorry," said Mr. Mycroft. "You must *feel* that smile, if it is to be any good to us. You see, we shall be watched while we are there, not merely by a couple of very shrewd if deluded human eyes. We shall be under the instinctive surveillance of hundreds of little detectives who will be judging us, not by our look but by our smell, and who will try to kill us the moment we seem sufficiently, or rather smell sufficiently, suspicious. You've heard about the 'smell of fear'? It's the adrenalin which fright puts into our sweat when we begin, as we say, to get into a cold sweat of fear, and, indeed, long before we know we are even feeling clammy. It is this smell which all animals, especially bees, find intensely provocative, and, if it gets strong, quite maddening. The bees we are about to visit are sufficiently crazy already not to be given the slightest further excuse for feeling provoked. It won't be much comfort to us if we are killed by their attacking us a little prematurely, according to Heregrove's plans."

"Oh, let me out of this," I broke in.

"No," he replied. "This, as you know, is the only possible line of safety. We must grasp this nettle. And the more we delay, the worse it will be; quite apart from the fact that Heregrove may strike again, if we give him any more time." Then the note of command changed to one of constructive assistance. "But I thought this necessary initiative against our enemy might require more of you than you could quite command at will. Whatever you might wish, and however necessary you might see it to be, I saw it might well be impossible for you to get yourself to feel that this is a fine, boyish adventure. And as you must believe this, as your part in our act, if you are to convince the greater part of our audience—and if they hiss us, we are lost—just swallow this. It's only benzedrine hydrate. Does no harm. Not a thing to live on, but it does pull one through little scenes like this and makes one's acting convincing."

I gazed with some misgiving at the small white tablet. I hate drugs. If I get into a mood I stay in it until it moves off. I don't believe in making efforts with oneself; after all, does one ever know what one is doing and why things go on inside oneself? But I suppose every criminal going to the scaffold gulps down willingly enough his small regulation tot of brandy, even though he has always hated the taste up till then. I got it down, and Mr. Mycroft kept me walking up and down for some time while he ran over our final dispositions. As he talked, it seemed to me increasingly clear that he was a master mind, Heregrove simply a malicious fool and that we had him in our grasp.

The mood held even when we found ourselves at his door and, if anything, grew even stronger when I listened while Mr. Mycroft took the whole game out of my hands and played it, I had to own, incomparably. All vestige of the leisurely old bore had vanished. He was as sparklingly vivacious and at the same time as charmingly ingenuous as a schoolboy. No doubt he was an amazing actor, but it was equally clear to me that he was really in high spirits, an old hunter, finding itself once again following a breast-high scent, a veteran adventurer looking once more into the bright eyes of danger. Romantic similes and well-worn ones, too, I know, but I must set down things as they happened, and that was exactly how I saw him then. It explains a little the extraordinary ascendancy he was able to have over me.

Heregrove, on opening, had not looked hospitable, though he pulled his face together and was obviously both determined to appear at his ease and uninclined to think that we looked dangerous or even suspicious. Obviously we did not. Here was that young fool who had already once put his silly head into the trap and now again, as stupid as a pop-eyed trout, which takes the same hook five minutes after it has got off it safe back into deep water, was returning for another visit to the man who was determined to murder him in cold blood. And he brings with him an old, capering zany, also after honey, and who also might serve well as Demonstration Case No. 3 of the perfect, trackless killer.

Mr. Mycroft was, as it happens, asking about honey. He had introduced himself and he had spoken with disarming frankness about his failure to keep bees himself. He supposed he hadn't the knack and was too old now to learn. His only wish had been to keep himself in honey. He had no knowledge of the strange insects and confessed that he found it hard to understand their normal ways, let alone their crotchets, their likes and dislikes and their complaints, of which there seemed to be no end and each one more mysterious than the last. Then his young friend here had told him that he had an acquaintance up at this end of the village who had kept him supplied for a long while now with excellent honey.

"Perhaps it's a breach of village etiquette for me to call. Each community has its rules, which the outsider must learn. So I persuaded Mr. Silchester to come along with me this afternoon."

There was nothing very cunning in the opening, but it was delivered with an indefinable air, with that quiet, cheerful assurance which creates an atmosphere in which the other side simply has to accept your initiative and to believe at its face value what you say.

"Oh, come in, come in," said Heregrove.

He was obviously having to give ground, as a man with a weaker wrist, poorer eye, and less skill has to yield ground to a more powerful fencer. I was surprised to find myself feeling that we were the attacking party, and Heregrove in danger of us, not we of him. We entered that dreary living room, and he made an effort, having landed us there, to get away.

"I'll just go down and get you the honey. It's at the bottom of the garden, as Mr. Silchester knows."

That appeal to me, somehow, gave another fillip to my still rising courage. I certainly now should not smell of fear as long as I realized that our enemy, however consciously still unaware, was subconsciously so uneasy that he had to call me in to confirm his right to get unsuspected away from an old, effusive man and a dolt of a young one.

Mr. Mycroft, however, was as quick as a fencer taking an opening of his enemy's guard.

"I spied your garden as we talked outside. I think, too, I noticed that you have some uncommon stripings on your tulips. I wish I knew as much of bees as I do about tulips. I will take a modest wager you have a very interesting mutation there. Perhaps chance aiding skill? The chromosome study of tulips, I confess, fascinates me."

With his rapid conjuror's patter, Mr. Mycroft gently, firmly irresistibly, forced his company on the retreating Heregrove. I followed, and so we three went down the garden path, up which I had last come so short a time before, little better than a fugitive and, as it happened, branded with the mark of death. When we reached the egregious bunch of late, mid-summer tulips—which, of course, I had never before noticed—Heregrove muttered something about knowing nothing about flowers, and indeed the flower beds fully confirmed him. But Mr. Mycroft would have none of this "false modesty," as he rallyingly called it.

"Obviously, my dear sir, you are not one of those wearisome, prettysome cottage gardeners, but, whether by luck or no, here is a plant well worth an expert botanist's interest. I can't claim to be that, but I can claim to be able to recognize a remarkable sport when I see one."

He bent, examined the plant, looked into the rather closely folded petals, at the anthers or stamens or whatever botanists call that sort of tonsil things which flowers have in their throats.

Then, suddenly, "But we are forgetting our honey," he said, straightening himself up.

Heregrove had stopped, standing closely beside him. He was quite clearly taken in by his apparently bona fide enthusiasm and quite as clearly at a loss how to manage this lively old bore and keep him at the proper distance from places where his long nose might scent things less sweet and harmless than the faint, clean perfume of the tulip.

"The bees are apt to be a bit cross now; frayed nerves at the end of the season." Heregrove tried to make a little joke of it. "You had better not come too near."

I thought he glanced at me in a questioning way. The next moment he strode off to the little shed. Bees were coming and going in the air, just over our heads, as they went to and from the hives. But none paid any attention to us. The moment Heregrove had turned from us, however, my lively old companion was seized with another idea.

"Bless my soul," he remarked, making off quickly across the garden, "if that isn't purple Pileus growing by that stable door. Of course it's not rare, but in this locality, any mycologist would be surprised. I must have a glance at it; perhaps a local variant."

Heregrove had turned round with his hand on the latch of the honey shed, one foot already over the door sill. When he saw dear, old Mr. Mycroft skimming across the paddock something far more like terror than rage swept his face. I stood in between looking from one to the other.

"Mr. Mycroft," he shouted, "come here!"

"Just a moment . . . Purple Pileus . . . Odd locality," floated back over Mr. Mycroft's shoulder.

Suddenly Heregrove, leaving the door of the shed open, bounded across the garden strip, passed me without a look, and started running toward Mr. Mycroft. I thought all was up—that he would kill both of us on the spot. I stood, of course, stock still. Action, it will now be clear, is not my role. I am quite a good observer, though, in spite of what Mr. Mycroft may think. I can see the whole of that scene as though I had a photograph of it lying before me now. Heregrove, as suddenly as he had begun to run, stopped and fell into a walk. That, I realized, must mean that he saw he would be too late. When he reached the stable door, Mr. Mycroft was coming out.

I heard his clear, vividly interested voice saying, "The spores have spread inside. The fungi are indeed the most interesting of all plant life. Of course, though, your tulip is the thing here. A high spot in my day. Thank you, indeed. Oh, you haven't yet the honey. You shouldn't have troubled to run over when I called, I'm always so excited by any plant discovery I make. Experts are too often like that, on their own subjects. It makes them bores, I fear. Ordinary, sane men can't understand all their enthusiasm—seems affected, indeed, almost insincere."

I could see Heregrove struggling with himself, but he had no chance of doing anything. Mr. Mycroft's ascendancy, the interpretation of our visit which Mr. Mycroft had forced on Heregrove's mind as the obvious truth, indicated precisely the same behavior which his own caution urged. He could not afford, I now saw, an outburst in front of two witnesses. I thought he would burst, though. As we parted, he was scarcely master of his voice, when, with the honey parceled up, we turned to go. He muttered the conventional courtesies and I could see the vein on the side of his forehead pulsing with its heightened pressure.

Out of earshot, Mr. Mycroft's first remark was not at all cheering, however.

"We shall have to call again."

"Couldn't you go alone, now you know him?" was my rather mean but really quite natural reply.

I was ashamed when I had said it and so quite a little relieved when, instead of taking me to task as he might, Mr. Mycroft's answer was merely, "The benzedrine hydrate is wearing off. You'll feel a bit let down now. As soon as we have buried this very dubious purchase in your garden, you had better turn in."

I felt even more ashamed when we went into the brick-walled part of my garden at the back of the house and Mr. Mycroft, with an energy I really could not command, proceeded to dig wide and deep the cursed honey's grave. When I wanted to stop, thinking we really had dug enough, for digging always makes my back ache, all he said was, "I have owed my life too often to not skimping jobs, to start doing so now."

At last, like bewitched gold, it was safe underground, and we were back in the sitting room, after washing in the kitchen.

"He's puzzled, and a bit frightened," Mr. Mycroft began. "But I'm puzzled, also, and if I depended only on the law to protect you and me, I'd be frightened too. There isn't a case against him, though of course he's as guilty as Judas and as dangerous as a cornered lynx."

"Didn't you get a clue in the stable?" I asked, almost irritably.

"A clue, yes," he answered. "But a clue is not a conviction, and the sharper you are at getting clues, the surer you may be that a jury will not see the strength of the evidential chain."

"But where are we, then?" I asked, with a growing sense of frustration.

"I'll tell you all I know. It may be more than you noticed."

"Of course it is," I said wearily. He bowed.

"Well, I hope you'll soon be comfortably asleep; but I must first clear your mind as to our present actual situation and our future action. First, I was determined to get into that house. Neither you nor perhaps Heregrove himself knew that that entry was forced. We walked in while talking and distracting him. If you keep on talking to a person who does not wish to talk, and meanwhile walk straight at him, as long as he thinks you are absorbed in what you are saying and aren't aware that you are walking him down, he moves back, thinking only how to stop you talking and so bring you to a standstill. So Heregrove, in spite of himself, had actually to say 'Come in.' Once we were in, Heregrove's next move, a fairly blind and un-thought-out reaction, was to keep us from getting into the back premises, the outhouses, etc.

"The room itself was just worth the visit. In one corner I saw a familiar puce-colored piece of paper. It is the cover (unmistakable to those who know it) of a queer foundation in the United States, which has much money, some brains, little judgment, and less method. It lives on the bequest of a millionaire who was abducted and held for ransom by some kidnapers, left nearly to die (and certainly to get fairly unhinged) by the official police, and finally was saved by a private detective whom I once knew. The detective's reward was a small fee, the foundation of this institute (the founding of which he, as far as his own interests were concerned, unwisely opposed, for millionaires even when sane *must* found institutes, as medieval barons had to found chantries and as hens must lay eggs), and the right to receive, all his life, copies of all the Foundation's publications.

"As I have said, I know that detective, and through him, I receive the periodical. The trust publishes research work for amateur detectives—a queer hobby, but more popular than you would suppose. And they have done some useful work—among a mountain of rubbish. As it happens, they were the first people to issue a description of the magnetized-dust test for fingerprints too faint to be picked up in any other way. They also published a very useful biochemical study of the animal ammonias. As we left the room I managed to see the number of the issue which he had. I will look it up when I get home, but I would take another wager that it is the issue which has that biochemical study in it.

"The next point, the tulip, was, of course, a bluff. His garden shows that he doesn't know enough even to know that I am fooling him. Naturally, I know sufficient genetics to counter him if he should try to expose me. He knows something about animal genetics and neglects plant genetics—the typical specialist; only in this case he has one confining aim—to perfect a new way of killing. No doubt he now does think he has got a freak tulip, and, as it happens, all these striped tulips are due to an interesting derangement of the chromosomes, as Hall has shown. But I turned to the tulip because it allowed me to examine not it but Mr. Heregrove at close and unsuspected range. A man changes his coat when he works in a laboratory but not his trousers. If he works long enough—and if he has no one to take his clothes to the cleaners, and it is obvious Mr. Heregrove has not—his trousers will get marked. Heregrove's trousers were within six inches of my eyes while I extolled that convenient but commonplace tulip, and I could see quite clearly a number of small stains and etches on the cloth which could be made by nothing but acids. So he makes his stuff himself. Next, I had to find out where."

"That's why you trotted off to the stable when he was almost in the shed?"

"Of course."

"But why should not his hellish laboratory be in the house? Isn't that more likely?"

"It is difficult to keep a horse in the house."

"I don't understand."

"It was plain to me directly you told me about the stable. Don't you know—we raised the matter before our visit to Heregrove, when we were discussing the smell of fear—that even amiable bees will often go mad if a sweating horse comes near them? You must never approach hives on horseback after a stiff gallop, unless you are looking for trouble. Heregrove's little research was naturally on the biochemical ammonias of horses. In other words, he has been looking for an essence which, when in full strength, will have just that quality which most rouses bees. He has (to put it in harsh Anglo-Saxon) been distilling and quintessencing sweats, like a medieval warlock, with all the witch-doctor's malignancy and far greater efficaciousness. His first simple experiment worked well enough to kill his wife walking in the garden. And now, like the first radio researchers, he is becoming ambitious to strengthen his transmission and to be able to make his messages travel over long distances. Your house is more than a mile away. It was just bad luck (or Destiny) that he didn't—well, shall we say, get perfect transmission."

"But you didn't find anything in the stable?"

I wanted to get down to facts. Mr. Mycroft could not be kept sufficiently interested in the real issue, that I was in danger and must somehow be got out of it. The problem, I could see, was to him one of general interest and my fate was only one feature in it. That was a point of view which perhaps I must understand but with which even he could not expect me to sympathize. He looked up, for he had been following his own line of thought, with his eyes fixed on the ground, and I expect he had really quite forgotten about me as a human being.

"No," he said, meditatively; "no, he has dismantled his laboratory. Not an uncareful man. I have known murderers as ingenious and far less careful—the two types do not necessarily go together. I could see where the bench and racks must have been. He was not lying to you when he said water was laid on in that stall. And after this visit of ours I am sure that a man who is as careful as that will take the precaution of clearing up again and even more thoroughly. And not only in the stable. The puce-covered periodical will go—would have gone already, but he was needing it right up to date and he did not expect we should get into the house, or if we did, that one of us would have such an out-of-the-way piece of knowledge as to be able to recognize that cover. All that remains, secreted somewhere, are a few small phials of a rather rank-smelling liquid marked 'Disinfectant'; certainly not healthy for microbes and certainly not very lethal, even if very nauseating to man. What good could a prosecution make of those, even should they be found?"

"Why," I shot in at this somewhat rhetorical question, for here I had direct experience he had not, "why, if the stuff was put on a piece of cloth and bees released near it, then you would see them go mad and bury their stings in it. Put a wretched rabbit in court with a smear of that stuff on its fur and it would be stung to death before the eyes of judge and jury! I can't think of a more conclusive demonstration and a more damning proof."

"You mistake our man," he replied without showing any interest in my contribution. "He's not so simple as that. In fact, I want you to realize that he is uncommonly clever, in his way—careful and cunning. No doubt he saw that was a way in which the noose might be slipped over his neck. I told you, at the beginning, that he bred special bees. True, he didn't know about their hearing and their curious limitation and ability to be controlled thereby. But that is just like nearly every specialist. Because he knows so much about their smelling reaction, he overlooks their hearing. He bred a curiously fierce and poisonous bee. You might expect that psycho-physical linkage—after all, rage is a kind of poison, and, no doubt, venom was evolved gradually by animals which, both weak and vindictive, were literally and bodily embittered by their sense of wrong and age-long yearning for revenge. There is, you know, a bee in Australia which, because it has no serious enemies, has yet to evolve a sting. The sting in all the bees and insects that we know is evolved from the ovipositor, the instrument first evolved just to insert their eggs into safe places. Venom is a late thing. There are, I gather, no poisonous snakes before the Miocene. It takes some considerable time and effort and brooding to be able to be as malignant as you wish. *Nemo repente fuit turpissimus.*"

"Yes, yes," I had to break in. "But we are discussing how *this* man got his diabolical knowledge and skill which today is making at least one of us go hourly in peril of his life!"

Mr. Mycroft did not seem vexed by my interruption, which, after all, considering his ranging interests, was necessary.

"Yes," he said," I was just coming to that. For though you might expect him to be able to blend fierceness with actual venom and to increase them together, I must own that his next breeding effort was remarkable and one which I might even have been inclined, offhand, to say was practically impossible. He refines animal ammonia, especially horse ammonia, until he gets a peculiar essence which wildly maddens a bee, but only a particular breed and strain of bees—in fact, his own monsters. No doubt his brooding mind caught that clue from what is known about those rare, but now well-noted and observed, peculiar specific affinities between the olfactory sense of one particular species of insect and the scent of one single species of plant—the best-known of which cross-alliances of insect and plant is, of course, the Yucca flower and the Yucca moth. But I mustn't say more tonight. You are dead tired."

It was true. I was having more and more difficulty in stifling my yawns when, however anxious I was to get out of the trap, he would give me long lectures on natural history. His next remark was, however, to the point and cheering.

"We certainly have at least one clear day for work, for Heregrove will spend tomorrow, every minute of it, re-extirpating every suspicious trace. I wouldn't wonder if he opened even the horse's grave and gave it another dose of quicklime."

That faintly awoke my interest to ask one casual question.

"How did the horse meet its death?" I questioned, as I showed him out of the garden gate.

"It was stung to death, poor brute, for demonstration purposes," he replied, and went off into the dusk.

7

DOUBLE-CROSSING DESTINY

In spite of such a day, a day alternately too exciting and quite tiringly boring, I slept, nonetheless, quite well. I certainly was hugely tired. But I saw I could not let things rest as they were. I was like a criminal with only a short reprieve, and I must act if I were ever really to be safe and free again. So as soon as I woke I was up, had my breakfast, and hurried off to Waller's Lane—not without an apprehensive look up the road which led in the other direction to the dreaded honey-snare.

Mr. Mycroft was already out in his garden and greeted me with, "The first experiment is over and as we expected. Look, I'll repeat it." At the end of a cane he had attached a pair of tweezers in which was a speck of cotton wool, oily and brown. He put it toward one of the alighting boards of his hives. The bees scattered and the working hum turned to a buzz, but, on the cane's being taken away, only a few followed it, half-heartedly, and they soon returned to work.

"Is that the stuff?" I asked, rather scared.

"Yes," he said. "You see, my mild Dutch don't like it, but it certainly does not make them homicidal. Now look at this."

He stepped back through the open French window into the house, returning with another similarly tipped cane. He advanced it to the hive and immediately there was quite an ugly commotion—a squadron swooping out after the offensive ferrule. He thrust it into a pot of water and, after some angry rushes and swirls, the squadron also returned to work.

"That was a fairly strong brew of ordinary horse-sweat ammonia. You see how clever our man has been! His insect only goes quite mad over a special brand of distillation, a brand which actually affects the normal bee *less* than ordinary horse sweat."

"But how did you get the stuff?" I asked, excitedly.

"Even the coolest, most thoughtful criminal makes a slip if you follow him carefully enough," he replied musingly. "You remember those young murderers Leopold and Loeb, of Chicago? They planned quite coolly and, as they calculated, quite completely, to murder that schoolboy and get away with it. And all their plans run according to schedule, well enough. But, while they are disposing of their victim's body, one of these creatures, who think they are so superior to human mistakes and weaknesses, actually drops his glasses on the ground and there they are picked up, for they are plain for any passerby to see. Within a couple of hours the Chicago oculists are all rung up, the description of these distinctive lenses given. The oculist who ground them looks up the specification in his files and Leopold and Loeb's names are in the possession of the police. Part of their minds must have heard those glasses click as they struck the ground, part of their attention have noticed them lying there while they looked around, approving their silly, sinister skill, seeing how well they had concealed their victim's body. But they were betrayed by that deep part of consciousness which they had disowned. We reckon ill who leave it out.

"Heregrove has done much the same. I did not tell you last night, as it might have made you sleep badly had you known that I had the deadly stuff on me. But I had, you remember, taken the precaution to bury the honey deeply, and, I believe, without their own honey to trail them to their victim, the vampire bees cannot find you simply by this ammoniac stuff. Once they have found you and you are marked—well, I have told you how happy I am you are alive and how lucky I think you are to be so. Here in this garden we are, anyhow, safe, for, if they should arrive, I can turn my siren song on them.

"But how did I get any of the stuff? Well, I have told you—because the clever criminal is just the man who makes a complete, amnesic slip every now and then, so that you have only to dog him long enough for him to let an utterly damning clue fall into your hand. I have only a little of his precious brew and that under strict glass-and-wax stoppering. The smirched scrap I showed the bees a moment ago I am now going to drop into my electric furnace where it will be ash in a moment."

He suited the deed to the word and I could hear the damp speck of wadding hiss just before he shut to the miniature furnace's door. He returned, picked out the first cane, twitched off its tip of sodden wadding so that it was flicked over the hedge, upset the pot of water with his foot, and, while he watched the dry soil suck up the damp, continued.

"The piece I picked up was in the stable. I had, as you know, only a moment to glance round and to see that the laboratory had been liquidated, and was just turning to meet Heregrove, for there was no use taking unnecessary risks by letting him come upon me gazing at the site of his hell's kitchen—when I saw a scrap of whitish cloth on the dark ground. I stooped, picked it up, dropped it in my pocket, and walked out with my toadstool patter to meet our enraged but nonplused host. I guessed in a moment what it was—the sham finger-bandage which he used as his not uningenious way of tainting you."

"But why wasn't it covered with bees?" I questioned.

"That," he answered, "is one of those points of psychology where, as on a wavering border line, reason touches instinct—instinct which isn't mechanic reaction or clear calculation, the two processes we know something about, instinct of which we know, in actual fact, nothing. This is the converse of the Leopold and Loeb question—why did their senses betray them? Here we have to ask, why does that blind instinct which makes the bee sting, till it ruptures itself, an object which insults its nose, suddenly yield to a kind of reason which tells it a rag can't suffer or at least can't be killed? True, they stung your coat but it smelled human and they were looking for you. But, after all, our real problem is the Leopold and Loeb side of the question. What non-reasoning power betrayed also our careful, calculating Heregrove? Of course, as soon as he had seen you off the premises he went to the stable. The bees were in by that time and he was safe. But still, as it was only just dusk, a few loiterers might be coming home late and he knew well that even half a dozen stings are probably fatal. So he drops the rag, probably washes and disinfects his hands in the stable—and then why doesn't he come back and take the rag to burn it? Probably he does mean to come when it is quite dark, so that he can be quite sure all the bees are in and also that no one will see him burning anything. He is as careful as that, and his place can be seen from the road, and, you see, all this taking care only maneuvers him into the position where the fatal forgetfulness can be brought into play. What we do know is that he did forget to come back and so we have hold of this invaluable rag."

"I don't see the rag is much use to us," I said. "It doesn't tell us anything we didn't know and won't help get us a conviction, as the glasses convicted Leopold and Loeb."

"It will do more for us," Mr. Mycroft replied.

"How?" I exclaimed. "How can it?"

His face went graver than I had ever seen it. He remained silent for a moment.

Then he said, "I wonder, Mr. Silchester, whether you could bring yourself really to trust me?"

That is the kind of question I can't help profoundly disliking. It seems to me rhetorical, melodramatic.

"When a couple of people get mixed up" (I was just going to say "by Destiny," but then that would make me also sound pompous and theatrical) "by luck in a mess with a lunatic, it seems rather silly to ask, when it's practically all over, whether one of them trusts the other."

"You take a far rosier outlook on the immediate future than I do, Mr. Silchester," he coolly replied, "if your considered opinion is that we are already almost out of this peculiarly tangled wood."

My heart sank. Before, it had always been he who had cheered me and I recalled with growing chill that though he *was* in danger, he was prospective victim No. 3 while I was No. 2 and No. 1 was long in her unavenged grave.

"We are," he went on, "at a place where two tracks divide. Our lives—I say it advisedly; I have often gambled with mine and I know something of mortal risks—our lives depend on whether the track which we decide to take is the right one. At the end of one of these trails there lies a peculiarly painful end for you and me, and" (it was this, I must own, that "put the screws on me") "and, Mr. Silchester, you have had a taste of this weapon which is now aimed at you as certainly as any gunman has ever aimed at and shot down his victim."

"Mr. Mycroft," I said in a voice which, though it may have expressed apology did express defeat, "I don't know why I am always trying to be difficult. I suppose it is because I am so frightened that I won't own I am, and so I try to get back onto that formal relationship which we should be on if this horrid secret peril had not forced us together."

How true that has proved—far truer than I thought even then. Mr. Mycroft evidently believed me.

"I don't want to frighten you needlessly, I think you realize. In fact, it is of the greatest importance that you should keep your nerve. Lose that and we may both be dead far sooner than we need be. But we must be quite clear about our situation and have no illusions over it. I have here the essence which, to put it frankly, even if it sounds melodramatic, puts death on people, at least in this locality. The law can give us no protection. But destiny has put this stuff in my hands. Fate made Heregrove drop the one thing which he could give us as an adequate defense against his attack; fate made him drop it and leave it where I could find it without his seeing me do so. Fate provided that I should have in the pocket into which I thrust it that small flask of the three strong essential oils with which I had anointed your fingers. No doubt that fact gave us an additional defense against any attack we might have suffered as I came back across the paddock with the stuff on my person. You must own that such an arrangement of events, although it would not have served us had we not been ready to avail ourselves of it, did make possible the present turn of events and that it does look as though, if a human may be so rash to say so, fate was, at least, not against us in this matter.

"Well, however that may be, and acting on the saw that Providence helps those who do not neglect to help themselves, when I got home I looked up my puce periodical. As I thought, it did contain that useful if recondite piece of work on animal ammonias—a piece of sound research which perhaps at present only two men in Europe and America happen to want—the one to commit, the other to stop an indefinite series of cruel murders. With these tables and the actual smearings on the rag, don't you see what we can do, what we can't do, and why I cannot do less than ask for your absolute confidence?"

I suppose subconsciously I suspected already the position into which he was forcing me—no, that's not quite fair, and I must be absolutely fair—I ought to say the position into which Destiny was forcing me, forcing us. I played for time, again.

"What *can't* we do?" I asked evasively.

It seemed better to know first what couldn't help us, for I might find a loophole there; before facing what we might have to do to help ourselves, to save ourselves.

"I needn't labor the point," he said, eyeing me with an embarrassing steadiness. "To this man, the law is no more than a fence to a yellow-fever mosquito. The law protects us from the sudden, unpremeditated violence of the untamed blackguard. It is helpless against the calculating malice of a man who patiently and deliberately studies to get around its limitations. When you have really faced up to the fact—I know it is hard for those who have lived protected lives to face such an actuality—that the law, the magistrate, and the village policeman are helpless to protect you, then you will be free to consider fully the unavoidability of step two: of doing what we can do."

He waited; after some unpleasant moments of silence, I must have showed some sort of assent, for he continued.

"I think you have been right in counting the cost and I am glad you have come to the same opinion as myself, only after mature thought. Right as it is, as well as wise, it is, of course, a very unconventional view. But we are, morally, precisely in the position that frontiersmen are placed when pushing out to the limits of a new country. We have to work the law ourselves and to make it run where, as yet, there are no rails. The law one day will catch up with this situation; then we shall simply tell the railway clerk where we want to be taken and he will see that we are conveyed. Today it is still, in such cases as these, a case of the sheriff's posse. We have to mount our own horses and under our own steam go after the criminal. It is, here, still the stage where every citizen must uphold and apply the law. You and I are the Western sheriff's posse. Fortunately we are adequately armed—"

"You don't mean that we have got to go like moonlighters and shoot through Heregrove's window some night?"

He saw that my protest was hardly sincere, in fact, only a prevarication, but he took it with perfect courtesy. I felt like a hooked fish making a desperate dash and splash, trying to get off on a false issue, and let by the fisherman, while it spends its strength, have the full run of the line, only to be hauled in when spent.

"My metaphor was clumsy," Mr. Mycroft apologized. "Of course, I only mean that we can and must counter Heregrove with nothing more than those instruments which he is attempting to use on us and which the law does not recognize as methods of murder—which, in fact, it dismisses as accidental 'acts of God' and not of malicious man."

That was, certainly, put as reassuringly as possible. I could, and must own did, dismiss from my mind the Wild-West sheriff simile. It certainly did not appeal to me, the recluse, to ride about avenging murders which the law chose to overlook. I am not a Red-Cross Knight. But I am an easily scared individual, and the one fact which remained, boring down into my consciousness and pushing me to lengths which otherwise I should have thought absurdly desperate, was my actual desperate situation. I made a final twist, however.

"All right," I said, with an air of having thought everything out to the end and seeing exactly how much would be expected of me. "All right, go ahead. I promise you I will never divulge anything of this. Obviously I shall want, quite as much as you, to keep my mouth shut."

"Thank you," he said, a bit dryly, I thought. My heart began sinking to new low levels. "That means, of course, that you will collaborate with me, for, while I can manage the technical part of this problem quite well by myself, I shall have to require your assistance at the end, in the practical application. We shall, may I repeat, have to call on Heregrove again."

Those last words, which I had dreaded most, were like a knell.

"Now, Mr. Silchester," he continued, in the same level tone, as though we had been planning a picnic, "I must go back into my laboratory. When you arrived I had started a couple of experiments and I must go and see how they are cooking. You, too, will want to think over our conversation, no doubt. Perhaps you would like to rest or read in my library. The singing of my pet birds in there will not, as you have tested for yourself, disturb you. I venture to invite and advise you to stay here; not only because we shall have several more things to talk over, which we can best do as soon as my experiments are finished, but also because I honestly believe that today you are safer here than in your own house."

"All right," I said none too graciously but he seemed quite content. He knew that my resistance was broken. I was his pawn; a hateful position, even if you are to be used to checkmate a man who wants to murder you.

The morning passed slowly. I could hear Mr. My-croft cluttering about, across the hall, in his laboratory. I couldn't read. I sat there dully, my mind slowly, like a mud-locked eddy in a stream, turning pointlessly round and round the events which had me snarled. At last my attention was caught by those silly birds as they hopped round their cage, stupidly safe, too stupid to know they were safe. As I looked, there they were, at it again, he singing silently and she listening enthralled. That soundless singing seemed to me all part of Na-ture's senseless arranging of things. Then, somehow, I had evidently gone too far in my disgust with every-thing. I realized how self-centered I was being, expect-ing the world to be made for me and to care for my fate; and how perverse I must be, for, after all, if I could have heard these birds squeaking away to each other I should only have been exasperated at the noise. I be-gan to smile at myself. I got up, went over to the cage, and was agreeably surprised when the birds, instead of stupidly fluttering in dismay, both came at once to the bars, heads on one side, evidently expecting me to give them something or to play with them. I am not good with animals—they either bore or frighten me—but I must say, I felt a sudden reassurance that if I had to be wholly in the hands and power of a stranger, that stranger should have been able to make birds not only trust him but trust strangers also. I was musing on that; it was sinking into my mind, for it was a thought I was ready to reflect on, the only pleasant one I had had for some time, when the door opened.

Mr. Mycroft said, "Lunch is ready. I have washed. You know the way to the bathroom from your last visit."

Certainly, too, the house was very neat and efficiently run. That gave me almost as much confidence as the birds' confidence in me. And lunch was even better than last time.

"Last time," said my host as we sat down, "it was, I fear, a very scratch meal. Today, as I hoped I might persuade you to stay, there can be a little more design in living. Like everything else, a menu depends on foresight, in taking time in time." We started with borsch—a soup I love but could never get Alice to make.

"It is really one of the simplest of the great soups," said Mr. Mycroft in answer to some such remark of mine, "and, you are right, one of the best. The Russians are fine eaters. Primitive peoples often retain keenness in certain senses which we are too busy and hasty to have preserved. Taste and sound both are primitive. *We* have chosen sight, and so all our world is now hardly anything but a visual world, as far as we can make it. Our painting is better than Russian painting, in consequence. Their music and food are far richer. We have accuracy, neatness, tidiness. We treat smell as something disgusting, and it goes from us. 'You smell' is never praise in our mouths. Jacob's praise of his son, 'The smell of my son is even as the smell of the fruitful field,' makes us smile with more than a flavor of disgust. Indeed, 'you smell' is most often a phrase of the deepest loathing.

"We have order, but lack copious creativeness. We are scentless and are becoming very restricted in our hearing. Accurate but without flair (notice that word, set, by the logical French, over against logical thought— smell in contradistinction from reason). Precise but lacking intuition. And the narrowing and starving of our apprehension goes on apace. Already color—the side of seeing which keeps us most in touch with the warmth of actual living, is being banished as not quite nice. 'Loud,' we call it when condemning it—again a revealing word. We borrow it from our hearing, and we are afraid, anaemically afraid, of any volume, any width and size in things. Nothing must be too robust; everything must be muted, lower. We pick our way, creep about. We must at all costs be refined, even to the extraction of every flavor and vitamin out of life's raw juices. Plenty is vulgar. Well," he laughed, "we can actually and at this moment do something to correct that shrinking error. What a good color, as well as taste, borsch has! Loud, of course, and of course you know, in topical illustration of our point, that the word 'red' in Russian is the word for color itself."

So he prattled on. His obvious wish to distract and entertain me, and the excellent way his food was planned to match and support his talk, did give me quite remarkable relief. I think that was the first time that I realized that a wise, cool, calculating, and brave man can show (a fact which I had never imagined before) his coolness, courage, and considerateness by a gay and clattering amusingness and a wonderful and quite sincere interest in small and general things. I had never thought that a really powerful and strong and (I hate the word) good person could be gay and even foolish. I now began to suspect that only the biggest people, perhaps because they are at times as impersonal as life itself, can be merry and funny right at the moment of crisis, with their minds made up and their senses all alert as a marksman's. They don't even do it, I began to feel, even to cheer us, though perhaps that starts them. They do it because they are so free of everything but the actual moment. I don't know how to put it, but I suppose they are as timeless as an animal; perhaps more so, as timeless as a plant or even a rock.

I don't know, even less, why I have put all that down. I think it is to make clear how it was that my mood, which had been pretty bad, changed into a sense of security and gaiety almost like Mr. Mycroft's. Surely that is remarkable enough to need some explaining?

"This luncheon," rattled on the host, "is to be a salute

to Russia: only red on the surface and at the dawn. Now we shall get down to the deeper Russia. Caviar, but not the cheap red. The sound black. This is also a pre-revolutionary way of serving it. I learned it when a Grand Duke of the *ancien régime* once wanted my company, hoping that together we might recover some rather indifferent pearls mislaid in a rather indiscreet way. That's a long story for lunch. Anyhow, I brought back this way of enjoying the sturgeon's black pearls. Cleopatra was right: most jewels would give us more real pleasure and do us in the end less harm if we could use them as crystallized cherries in a cocktail or a cordial, or as jujubes we could suck.

"Now for something more solid. These big Russian meat pies act as a pivot on which the meal turns, and they are wonderfully healthy if taken with their appropriate drink. This vodka was, I now recall, a present from that same Grand Duke who now, poor fellow, probably cleans boots in Paris or New York—so, I suppose, as I got the vodka, he must have got back the pearls. I hope they proved one of his liquid assets when the crash came. This is another sort of liquid which he certainly could not have got away with; so we need not mind using it ourselves. We will drink to his health, though, and to our success."

I felt now we could not fail, and drank to a success of which I was already unquestionably sure, though even that surety grew stronger as the warming stuff went through my veins. There followed a wonderful sweet: all of cream and almonds and honey. To a man as fond of sugar as myself it closed a banquet perfectly.

8

WASP STRIKES SPIDER

As we sat over our coffee, I therefore experienced no shock when Mr. Mycroft; without any change of his bright and almost careless tone, remarked, as though we had been discussing it all through lunch, "We'll pay that second visit to Heregrove this afternoon. The morning's work went perfectly—even quicker and better than I had dared to hope. Just come into the laboratory, and I'll be able to show you everything and how ready we are now to finish off this troublesome little matter."

One side of me knew that he was talking about a desperate and even illegal adventure. But that side was simply timid, calculating, bloodless reason. He had put his own mood into my blood, and that was surging about in a state of merriment which actually made (I must record it) the word adventure, to me, Sydney Silchester, have almost a ring of attractiveness in it, instead of the very warning sound which I have always connected with such a noun.

Mr. Mycroft closed the laboratory door, drew out a chair, cleared it of books, offered it to me, and himself perched, like a powerful bird, on the edge of the bench. Swinging round, he picked up a corked phial, drew the cork carefully and handed it to me. It contained, I should say, a egg-spoonful of liquid—quite clear but oily.

"Smell that," he requested.

I expected a shock to my nose and only sniffed as lightly as possible. I saw him smile, and so put it right under one nostril; then I drew a deep breath and finally almost touched the end of my nose on the test-tube's rim. Still I could smell nothing.

"Perhaps it's the vodka, or the garlic in the pie that has spoiled for the present my sense of smell," I said, a little apologetically, for though, or perhaps because, I hate all stenches, I rather pride myself on having a keen appreciation of scent.

He smiled back.

"I had noticed that you have an uncommonly lively olfactory sense. When we first came in here on your pristine visit you didn't like the laboratory smell, for you began to breathe through your mouth, though you made no effort to clear your nose, which you would have done had it been simply a little turbinal congestion which was temporarily troubling you. Then, when we went into the library, almost unconsciously, as we passed, in coming out, those Turgeniev novels bound in Russian leather— another reminder of my ducal devoirs—you could not resist just touching them and carrying your fingers immediately to your nose to relish the faint perfume."

"Then why—" I said.

"Because," he cut in, "there isn't any! That is just the point of my test. This stuff, I tried out on you. You have an uncommonly keen nose and you—scent is very 'suggestible'—expected to be able to detect, expected to be shocked by the strength of, a very rank odor. And you notice nothing. Try again, and don't touch the rim."

I snuffed until I must have vacuum-cleaned that glass, but not a ghost of a perfume rose to me.

"What does this mean?" I asked.

"It means," he encouragingly, if rather cryptically, remarked, "that we are far safer than anyone would have imagined that we could be. We have something amounting to the cap of invisibility."

"But what is it?" I asked again.

"Well," he said, "as it happens, it is that brown, pungent, so-called disinfectant, with which both you and I have been in touch."

"It isn't," I blurted out, "or, if it is, it has had taken out of it all the particular smell which made the original so dangerous."

"To us, yes, and that's half the battle: that's the defense, the parry. Your keen nose catches nothing. Mine isn't blunted. I have tried to keep my fivefold endowment sharp on every point of life's sacred pentagram. And scent, like taste, often outstays the present approved senses such as sight and hearing—on which our unbalanced age puts nearly all its weight. I, too, can smell nothing."

"But is there anything else to the stuff?" I prompted.

"We can't judge," he began.

"Then what's the use?" I exclaimed.

Having made up my mind to adventure, having thrown caution to the winds and with my courage seeming now unshakable, I experienced a sudden sense of impatience at all this caution and dawdling. But he cut me short.

"I didn't ask you in here simply to confirm my strong feeling that this essence is scentless. You must see that it is positive as well as negative."

He corked it carefully again, put the phial in the rack, anointed cork and glass with what my nose told me was his triple off-scent-thrower, the valerian, citronella, aniseed mixture. Next he told me to wash my hands as he washed his at the sink and then dabbed our fingers with surgical alcohol, rubbed them hard, and gave them also their anointing. That done, he went over to the other side of the room where there were some small drawers, their fronts covered with fine wire mesh, pulled out one, picked up a forceps, slipped back a trap, and brought out the forceps with a bee held by the wings.

"I captured it yesterday, in the early morning, before your Alice called for me. A few pirates were reconnoitering and a small squadron swooped. They'll never leave us alone, or any bees, as long as they are alive. I stunned them with sound, as you know, and picked up the few who actually fell on the lawn. They are now all dead except this one, though I gave them fine quarters and plenty of food. That, of course, is another mystery of the hive; it is what makes one of the greatest French apiarists say that the bee is not an individual, but only a loose, floating cell of that largely invisible organism or 'field' which we call the hive and of which we are able to perceive only its material core—the honeycomb and the queen.

"Certainly they will not live if kept from their swarm; and these are no exception. In fact, like most products of fancy breeding, they are evidently in this respect, as in others, more highly strung, more hysterical."

While he spoke he carefully carried the pinioned bee across the room. It, too, was obviously on the verge of death. Its legs moved slowly as if tangled in some invisible web. The antennae drooped. The bright, many-faceted eye already looked dulled. Mr. Mycroft put it down on the bench. It nearly fell over on its side, and then recovered itself; it began to crawl laboriously, blindly ahead. But it had to stop, out of what was obviously sheer exhaustion.

"Yes, its minute, invisible pipe-line to its mysterious source of its general life is nearly severed," he said, looking at it.

"It will be dead in a few minutes," I concurred.

"Still," he said, "we are taking no risks," and, rather unnecessarily, I thought, he spent a moment in securing the wings, by slipping with a fine brush a drop of spirit-gum under each wing and so sticking the wing to the body.

So moribund was the insect that it did not even buzz nor seem to feel that its wings were now glued tightly to its back. Mr. Mycroft waited until the gum had set. The bee remained still. Indeed, the only sign of life was that it did not roll over. I was watching it with considerable curiosity and carefulness, so that I did not see what Mr. Mycroft was doing. What I did see was that suddenly, for no apparent reason, the dying bee literally sprang to life. It was as though an electric shock had struck it. Perhaps no electric current could so have galvanized it. The whole small body seemed to swell, the drooping antennae writhed like tiny snakes. A vibration of such intense energy went through it that the wings tore themselves free from their sealing, leaving the veined, transparent vans still stuck to the back. The stumps whirred wildly. Luckily for us, the possessed mite could not rise. The frantic tremor pulsed through it again. The body curled over on itself in a paroxysm of violence, and it was dead. The body still remained upright and humped as it had died.

I looked up. With rubber stalls on both index fingers and thumbs, Mr. Mycroft was corking the phial again.

"Why doesn't it fall over?" was all I could find to say.

He answered me by picking up the forceps again and taking hold of the dead bee. It required quite a considerable pull, however, to raise the body from the bench. When it came away, there, quite clearly, was the long murderous sting torn from the body and left deeply buried in the hard-wood.

"The master passion strong in death," he remarked, dropping the curled-up little husk into the ash-bin under the bench. With his free forceps picking out the sting from the wood, he dropped it into a small crucible glowing red-hot above a bunsen flame.

"One thorn of experience is worth a whole wilderness of warning," he continued, "and demonstration is always necessary. We both now know beyond any doubt that in that test-tube we have something which is precisely what we must have—a thing the essential nature of which is quite impossible to be perceived by us, while to the particular bee which we have to circumvent, it is as flagrant as a cup of vitriol."

"And now?" I said.

I realized that the time had come when we must go ahead, apply our knowledge and free ourselves and the world of a deadly pest. I knew that by an hour or so of resolute and obedient action I should somehow be delivered from a living nightmare and be able once again to go back to my quiet, secure, happy life, into the steady sunshine from under this hideous cloud. I felt also a curious sense of assurance, which the demonstration had at least given me reason for—the feeling, I suppose, that a hunter, concealed in a tree and armed with the latest sporting rifle, must experience when, all unconscious that it is covered, a man-eater strolls into perfect range. I felt that our enemy was as powerful, as malignant, and as stupid in his vain ignorance of what he was up against, as a tiger. So it was not any longer timidity which made me hesitate.

I was hunting for words, though, when Mr. Mycroft, who had been with great care drawing the clear liquid out of the test-tube by means of a pipette-nosed flask, his task finished and test-tube and flask shut into a hermetically sealed drawer, looked up at me, remarking, "The chemical interest of this experiment (and, I own, that has been quite absorbing in its way) has not made me forget that this problem, though now solved materially, remains morally a very grave one."

So saying, he went across the room, throwing wide the window as he passed, and opened one of the

wire-covered drawers at the room's end. A dozen or so
bees flew out. I ducked, but they made straight for the
window. Looking out, I saw them swoop toward and
enter one of the hives on the lawn.

"They are glad to get home," he said, looking after
them. "I hate distressing them, blind and obsessed as
all bees are, imprisoned in their fossilized dream of instinctive service to the hive. Perhaps I need hardly tell
you that time and again while I was making this ex-
tract—eliminating the coarse essential oils, which alone
our crude olfactory nerve-ends can pick up; finding the
actual essence, partly by help of that odd article and its
tables and partly by testing out my various refinings—
by using that small caged party of my own placid bees
as tasters, or smellers, by watching the way they first
reacted and then, as the brew became specific they became almost unaware, when the stuff, then crystal clear,
brought near the pirates' detention drawer, made them
nearly beat themselves to death against their wire-gauze
bars—all that time the moral problem hung like a vast
cloud on the horizon of my thought. Then, as the material problem was completely cleared out of the way, I
turned on this other, and, to me, greater problem and
found my mind as clear, as made up, and as convinced
of its essential correctness as I am that the essence we
hold is the stuff we need to fulfill our purpose."

"What's your solution?" I asked. I was myself so

puzzled that I was really willing to take advice and act on it.

"I see," he said, looking at me, "you are kind enough now to trust me, so I am going to ask you one more favor."

I must have registered some dismay, for he quickly added, "It is a very small one and between ourselves."

He's going to seal me to secrecy, I thought. Well, we are certainly in the same boat. I had told him I should be silent. I would certainly promise again. Even if I were an inveterate gossip, this was the one subject for which my silence could be trusted.

I was, therefore, surprised when he said, "I am going to ask you to trust me enough not to ask as yet how I have solved the moral problem, but to adopt my solution. It will, I believe, help the difficult and still quite sufficiently dangerous parts we have both to play if the man whom we have to *try* cannot see any signs, however involuntary, of collusion between us. I have to convince him again, after having shaken him badly, that I am what he still on the whole believes me to be, so that he will dismiss me as only a possible and peculiarly defenseless victim."

Well, it was a relief to follow, not to have to make up one's mind, to know that here was an authority who would accept the responsibility both for the material arrangements and the moral consequences. Perhaps I was too sanguine, too suggestible. Certainly my mood of physical readiness and mental acquiescence was not normal. I learned that later. It is, I think, a point of considerable importance, for it makes me far less responsible should any trouble arise in the future.

All the while he was talking, Mr. Mycroft was making preparations with a definiteness and a precision which, I must say, kept my sense of assurance from waning; for he evidently foresaw his moves (whatever these might be) as clearly as a chess player of champion rank sees, as the end-game begins, the exact positions his pieces will take up to bring about the checkmate. There was nothing unexpected in the flasks being taken out of its drawer now that all the bees were gone and the window was up again. He wiped the nozzle of the pipette duct with spirits, fitted its small cap on it tightly, and then slipped it into his pocket. The next move, however, was puzzling. He went to his filing shelves and collected from a number of periodicals a couple or so of loose pages, placing these in a drawer near the window. Then he looked at his watch.

"We are not rushed for time. We shall not leave here until 5:30. Timing is, however, important. We must arrive when the sun is low, but it must not be dusk. Still, you always have to give these village craftsmen time. So I said three and, as I supposed, it is now four. I would rather none of us went down to the village. We ought not to be seen on that errand. I left my commission when I returned from you in the gloaming last evening. But though old Smith is slow, I think he will turn up. I am pretty sure he will have done the task I set him and I know he will be silent. He's the sort that likes a secret piece of fun, all the more when he has no clear idea what it is all about."

Naturally, I had no more notion than the unknown Smith as to the drift of these remarks. "A piece of fun" sounded almost the most inappropriate description that could be given of our adventure. Silence fell between us and while I was thinking of some way of trying to find out what he had meant, and beginning, even, to wonder whether he could have been so mad as to make a confidant of an outsider, I heard a limping step outside.

Mr. Mycroft went at once to the door, shutting it behind him; so I heard only a muffled word or two in the hall. The steps withdrew, and Mr. Mycroft returned, looking at a sheet of paper. I could just see that it was of quarto size and had a printed heading with a good deal of detail on it. After taking it and spreading it carefully on a drawing board which stood by the window, he turned it upside down so the heading, though well out of my eyes' range for reading, could now be seen running like a big footnote on the page. Holding it like this, with his free hand he opened the drawer in which he had put the loose pages and brought out what seemed a similar sheet, though with more writing on it; and this he placed wrong side up and a little above the first sheet. Then, taking a pen, he remained absorbed for some five minutes or so while he made what was, as far as I could judge, a small etching across what was now the top of the inverted sheet. He considered it a moment, compared it with something on the other sheet, and then went so quickly out of the room that I was unable to get a glance at it when he hurried by me. While I waited, I thought I heard the clack of a typewriter for a few moments, but was not sure.

He returned with his hands empty, simply saying, "Now we are ready. We have just time for a cup of tea. It is waiting us in the library."

We drank in silence. I knew I was at a divide in my life, but my mood remained curiously set, and, as I swallowed the tea—for, after all, tea is one of the most comforting of drinks—I actually felt the enterprising temper begin again to assert itself. When Mr. Mycroft said, "We ought to be getting on," I felt a curious mixture of two sensations. The one was like what I used to feel when taken by an uncle I liked to the Zoo. He knew one of the keepers in the lion house, so that we were let in behind the public cages and saw the keeper stroke a leopard. It was so pleased that it was both purring like a cat and at the same time tearing great splinters with its contracting claws out of the log on which it was sprawled. The other feeling I remembered experiencing when at school I was sent in to bat: everyone thought I should be bowled at once, but I actually hit a boundary and made twenty-three runs before I was stumped.

I do not recall what Mr. Mycroft talked about as we walked along, but a general impression remains that, like most powerful actors, he was building up his part. (I recall wondering whether that might have been his profession before he retired, and that after all he had not been a doctor. He certainly had a quite unusual and extraordinarily convincing way of taking parts.) I could not help seeing that now he was sinking himself into the character-mood he meant to impose on his audience; although that audience would only be two puzzled and more than a little uneasy men—one not knowing what kind of act he was going to put on but knowing that it was an act, and the other not knowing even who he was, but suspecting that he might be a fraud. I realized how much depended on his being able to put over that conviction of his actually being the part he was going to play—that this was so vital that even his play-acting must, in its detail, not be known even to me. For otherwise I would be prepared for his various actions, and my awareness of what was coming might destroy that sense of naturalness and spontaneity which he had to create, and which I, with my real ignorance must, and could only so, second.

I remember vaguely that he prattled about flowers and used a lot of technical terms. I don't think he intended me to listen. I know I didn't. He sailed up to Heregrove's door, seeming to pay no attention to the house, for he was apparently still engaged in a vivacious conversation with me, or rather pouring out an excited story into my uncomprehending ear. He would say frequently, "I was right. I thought I was—knew I was. And yet who would think it! I simply couldn't wait. Nor could he; nor would they; and you realize what that means! You don't surprise men like that into action unless you have a prize find—a perfect natural-history-museum piece."

We were at the door and he had rapped gaily on it, turned his back on it, and continued chuckling and repeating in a raised, excited voice.

"Yes, yes, Mr. Heregrove will be pleased at this; this means a tidy profit, if he cares for that, as well as no little distinction. The rights are all his. I have, of course, given him every credit, and I'll see he gets it. Most necessary to encourage amateurs, most necessary. The amount of good work lost by not doing so! Simply hopeless! Amateurs are always making discoveries and the professionals are too jealous to let the real finder have the credit."

He swung round in the middle of his stream of high-pitched chatter and struck the door again a couple of sharp raps. There was no reply. No pause came in his flow of one-sided conversation; no sign showed in his beaming face, as he scanned mine or played with an envelope in his hand, that he was impatient, that he was actually pressing to his lair a desperate criminal who was probably lurking within earshot. I do not think he had to keep the mask on by anything which I should have called self-control. All his surface self now *was* the amiable, excited old zany. Only, deep behind any detection, looked out the unsleeping vigilance which was determined that its prey should not escape it. I saw how right he had been not to tell me, an inexperienced actor at best (though I had taken quiet parts at school and once did quite a good Portia), and certainly not incapable of stage-fright on this awkward "appearance," not to let me know in any detail, the part he was to play. All the better could I fall in with my role, which, it was now clear, was to be the quite obviously mystified young man compelled to bring up again this absurdly eccentric old scholar. Collusion between us, not even a hunted murderer could suspect.

Suddenly, in the midst of one of these excited repetitions, he literally shot off at a tangent, skimming away from the door and round the corner of the house. Before I could follow I heard him cry, "Ah, you're here. Of course you would be. There were we, expecting to find you in the house. But you've guessed my news."

At that point I myself reached the corner of the

house and could see down the garden. Mr. Mycroft was waving a piece of paper in Heregrove's face—a face in which quite clearly a very dangerous look was simply being forced off by what in any other situation I would have had to call comical dismay. Quite obviously he had thought he was trapped. He had seen us approaching— had lurked in the house and then had stolen out to the back. For what desperate throw I did not like to think, but Mr. Mycroft had been too quick for him, must have heard his careful steps on the path and had run round to meet and balk him. The sun was level, the air already cool, the garden still, the hives silent. The queer, desolate place in that quietude had a strange, resigned beauty, as of someone who has decided that death is coming and who no longer dreads or questions it.

This sense, however, was certainly not in Heregrove's mind. What I can only call a sort of exasperated relief was springing up in him. He could not prevent himself from believing in the story which was being forced on him and in the character of the story-teller, who, even in his play-acting, was so much more powerful than his vain, mimicking, murderous, megalomaniac self.

"Ah," said Mr. Mycroft, wheeling round as I came up, "I have given poor young Mr. Silchester such a time! He's my senior in the village and he said I simply could not go forcing myself on you again. You would call, and then I might return your call. If there was anything pressing I could write. But I simply could not wait. It wasn't fair to you. You must know. The big people hadn't hesitated; had been pressing. 'Why,' I said, 'why, Mr. Silchester, Mr. Heregrove would never forgive me for delay, and rightly, rightly.' Formal courtesy can be real unkindness, when good news is being withheld—simply for punctilio, for nothing else!"

I stood by, the picture of that confusion which I felt, though feeling it for utterly different reasons than Heregrove, when he eyed me, concluded. It was quite safe for me to look at him. I *could* only register what he *must* misinterpret. So I watched his face with a curious sense of my own impropriety, at the horrible incongruousness of the whole scene. I even found myself smiling in a sort of weak, sheepish way, which of course was the most convincing piece of acting possible in the circumstances. Yet it rose in me spontaneously while I watched Heregrove's face change from the desperate look of the hunted to the cruel assurance that he was, again, the hunter; that, far from confronting implacable hounds, he was faced by a couple of insane hares gamboling right up to the place where he, the fox, lay hidden.

By this time Mr. Mycroft had forced his piece of paper, so that Heregrove was actually holding it and being made to read it.

"Directly I got back last night I felt I must tell the

big-wigs," ran on Mr. Mycroft. "So, though I dislike
long-distance calls, I rang up Miles. He knows I wouldn't
do that—at his home, too—unless I had real news. I told
him exactly of your find. For, to tell you the truth, Mr.
Heregrove, I shall never bring myself to believe that that
was chance! I know chance is said to be capable of making monkeys compose all Shakespeare by simply strum-
ming typewriter keys; but I never could believe that,
and anyhow, even for that, I understand, it is postulated
that they shall have infinite time. Well, well, we haven't
that," he went on, breathlessly. "Nor did Miles think so.
See, he wrote this note and ran out at once and posted
it so I should get it this morning. Miles knows! And as
he's been so long Secretary, a man in such a position can
speak pretty definitely for the Council. He knows their
mind and when they haven't one, he is it! And, see what
he says."

He went on craning over Heregrove's shrinking arm
and tapping the paper with his finger.

"'Full recognition . . . Not only valuable but important' . . . very scientific that, very. Knows the £s.d.
worth of this, but the scientific prestige is, of course,
the thing. *Tulpia Heregrovia* will be in all the catalogues
in a couple of seasons. You will have name and remu-
neration. Well, I expect you will value both, and in this
case both are comfortably considerable. The Dutch are
being forced off our market by these virus restriction

regulations. There's a demand now for really new mutations, a demand which makes bulbs fetch really big prices. A daffodil bulb raiser near Hastings had a sport worth £500. Tulips go higher, and once you have one, you may have many, if you have, as it is clear you have, the hand for that kind of thing. You see the Institute offers you all facilities. You know it, no doubt. No better place to work. They have sponsored many a brilliant amateur like you and, if I may so put it, set him up in a highly thriving way. Why I was so precipitate is that the Council meets tomorrow. You see, Miles mentions the date. He feels as I do. At this quarterly meeting they make the grants-in-aid for new research and offer their laboratory equipment and expert assistance, greenhouses, and planting-out plots to selected amateurs. If we can telephone Miles tonight that you accept, it will be a feather in both our caps—to have found a brilliant amateur grower who did not even think of applying to the Society!"

Mr. Mycroft ran off into asteristical chuckles—if I may coin an adjective—beaming alternately at the paper and at Heregrove's face.

"Dear old Miles," he ruminated, while evidently expecting at any moment Heregrove's affirmative. "You have, no doubt, seen that famous sign manual? It can do a lot, oh, quite a lot; though, as I always tell him, it is a hybrid sprung from an arabesque crossed with an anagram, and the only use of it is not to convey a name but to foil a forger. Well, I may telephone, 'yes,' mayn't I?"

Heregrove was obviously completely bewildered. The story, supported by the letter, he could not refute or reasonably doubt. But it was clear to me that though he believed the story, he was determined to refuse the offer, however profitable he felt it might prove and however firm he was convinced that it must be.

"You see, Mr. Mycroft, as I have told you, I am not interested in flowers. I am ready to believe you and Dr. Miles, that I have something valuable here. Perhaps—" (and here I saw lying creep across his face) "perhaps I did not tell you the whole truth last time and I have a certain knowledge and taste for flower breeding. But I cannot leave here or go up to London or attend the Institute. That is quite impossible. I'll sell the plant outright, if we can find an impartial opinion to decide its price. But I have other, more important interests than raising new varieties of plants."

I caught a certain contemptuous defiance and assurance in that last phrase. He was so certain of himself and his security that he was ready to tell us that he had more important work on hand than getting quite a considerable reputation and cash return. He was enjoying, even at a small risk of making us suspicious as to what that interest actually was, the tragic irony of telling us to

our faces that killing us was more sport for him and of
deeper delight than making new forms of life.

"I am sorry," said Mr. Mycroft, "I am indeed sorry
that we cannot persuade you to take this line."

His voice expressed real regret. It convinced
Heregrove, but, again, he was correct in judging the *expression* as being sincere, and hopelessly, fatally wrong
in estimating the reason for that sadness. He thought
he was faced by a fantastic, fanatical fancier, trying, all
unconsciously, to make a tiger come into the house and
play with a ball of wool. He was, in actual fact, face to
face with his judge who was pleading with him to take
a last chance—if, as it seemed to me, it was a spurious
offer—to escape his doom. It was appallingly thrilling to
me, this scene, which, with its tragicomic irony, seemed
to me, as I watched it, to be more terrible than any trial
scene, when the dry-mouthed prisoner at the bar sees
the judge put on the black cap.

I could not foresee how it was to end in detail. But
I could see that, however fantastic the dressing of the
parts, perhaps because of that element of fantasy—because the doomed man thought himself to be the perfectly disguised and quite compassionless dealer of our
dooms and that the man who pleaded with him could
by no possibility be doing what he was actually doing—
pleading with a murderer to turn from his way and
holding over that murderer his secret and his fate—be-

cause the murderer looked with now obvious contempt at the man he was driving to condemn him, thinking that that man, his judge, was simply a helpless old fool and the murderer's victim No. 3. I could see more than the immediate crisis.

Because of this terrible ignorance, this complete, hopeless misapprehension of his situation, the scene suddenly filled me with an overwhelming sense of its general significance. Here in this grotesque play of stubborn misunderstanding, black hardheartedness dooming itself, and mercy pleading, as it only could, and maybe only can, in disguise and under symbols, in some way all our human tragedies, all mankind's doom, seemed to be performed before me at that moment in miniature. I was shaken more deeply than by this one savage and cunning brute's disaster. It shook me because I recognized suddenly, and terribly vividly for the moment, that this situation is in some way what we all confront in life: those people and events which we treat most contemptuously and thoughtlessly are just those which, watching us through their mask of insignificance, plead with us to understand and feel, and failing to impress and win us, have no choice but to condemn us, for we have really condemned ourselves. I own I cannot recapture that feeling, but in honesty I must record these thoughts which then went through my mind.

"Well, well." Mr. Mycroft's crestfallen voice broke a

silence which cannot really have been long but which to me seemed to have been indefinite—a queer, timeless interlude between two acts of our dangerous farce. His eyes had been fixed on Heregrove, with an intensity which I could interpret as a supreme interest; scientific curiosity blended with a high compassion, and which Heregrove, as confidently, had to mistake for an unbalanced obsession with some trivial specialty. Heregrove took the first step, however.

"I am busy, gentlemen, and, as I can't agree to your suggestion, I must say good evening."

Then, grudgingly, and not to seem too suspiciously contemptuous, it was clear, he added in a perfunctory voice, "I'm obliged to you for calling my attention to the possibility."

He began to turn away, but quite easily and in character, Mr. Mycroft fell in beside him, ambling along down the garden path, carrying his way and imposing his company with that renewed flow of rapid talk.

"A real disappointment. Perhaps you couldn't accept, I realize. But I know *you* realize it was kindly meant and am sure you are interested in what I shall still call your achievement. Rewards you may neglect, but research, I think, you will permit? Ah, there it is! You will, I know, allow me one more examination. The last was little more than a glance—just enough to make sure, not enough to appreciate. We collectors and breeders, Mr. Heregrove, you cannot imagine how each minute variation and mutational clue thrills us. What the layman hardly remembers—indeed, scarcely notices—thrills us as a new star thrills an astronomer."

We had come abreast of the few tulips which Mr. Mycroft's skill had somehow turned into a pivot on which he made revolve his whole delicate and dangerous operation.

"As a breeder yourself, I need hardly tell you," he continued, addressing Heregrove, who stood by uneasily with obviously rising savage impatience, but unable to see how at that moment he could break away, "I shall take no liberties with your treasure, a treasure no doubt not less valuable than the ever-famous black tulip. But," and Mr. Mycroft bent toward the largest of the blooms, "I know you will permit. . . ."

He paused as though absent-mindedly engrossed in peering into the petals, but really, I could see, to be certain that he had excited and held the cupidity of the man, who, whatever his dreams of avarice and wealth won from murder, was still certainly very hard up. Heregrove, who, it had seemed a moment ago, would break clean away or at least stroll ahead, was caught, coming closer, lured and drawn as a trout is drawn in a curve by the fine line of the dry-fly fisherman, and himself also looking now, rather stupidly, I thought, at the flower.

I think that was the first time that I had realized, while I was up against him, that after all, with his considerable cunning, he was really a stupid man. One had only thought him terrible and all-knowing because one was frightened oneself and so could not put oneself in his shoes. Nearly all murderers, I began to see, are terrible only because we fear them and appear clever only because of the short start which breaking the rules gives them. We begin by thinking they are ordinary persons and won't violate the regulations of the game and so they get a lead for a stroke or two.

"I know you will permit me," Mr. Mycroft absent-mindedly repeated, "to study the plant closely."

Heregrove's eyes went from Mr. Mycroft to the flower and back again. Obviously he was getting every moment more confused. In his muddled mind the notion which seemed to have a small but unworking majority was that Mr. Mycroft was about to snatch the precious bloom from its stem and go skimming down the path with it. I, apparently, was cast by him for the role of the interceptor, who by blundering into the path of pursuit allows the thief to make a clean getaway. Mr. Mycroft added still further to the man's confusion by bending so far forward that he balanced himself by putting his hands behind his back. The rape of the bloom was quite impossible in such a position, a position in which Mr. Mycroft looked like a giant jackdaw as he turned his head and looked up with a keen eye at Heregrove.

"Yes," he said. "As remarkable as I thought. But the light is failing and the petals are heavily contracted. I have seen enough to memorize the principal features for a brief account—which I shall, of course, submit to you. And, if I might advise, I would suggest that you register your find as soon as possible. If you don't by any chance know the address, I will give it to you as we leave."

This stroke evidently persuaded Heregrove that there was something to be got out of us, at practically no trouble to himself; that we might actually yield a little profit alive before yielding him the experimental interest of our deaths. So Mr. Mycroft prepared his next stroke until nothing could have seemed more natural and unsuspicious.

"The bulb is, of course, the thing, and as no one but ourselves knows about it, it is as safe in the ground as buried treasure. So I know you won't mind, so as to save a second visit to a busy man, if I take the one thing which is needed to make the full description of your wonder—a few grains of its pollen. They can, of course, be of no commercial value and are only of purely scientific interest."

I saw that Heregrove knew enough of flowers to know this to be true and that he thought he had better assent so as to conclude the interview. This would be the quickest way of getting rid of us. He may even have grunted permission. Anyhow, he stood still, looking down while Mr. Mycroft's hands unlocked from behind his back. His right hand was hidden from me, for I was on his left, a few yards nearer the house, and already the light was not of the best. I saw him put something into the bell of the flower and then heard him give a slight exclamation of annoyance.

"It's blocked," I could hear him saying almost to himself. Then, to Heregrove, "These patent pollen-extractors respect the flowers' virginity but I am not sure that the old toothpick with a speck of cotton-wool on the end wasn't better. It was certainly less trouble. These superfine tubes are always getting congested. I must blow it out." He turned and I could see in his hand the flask, the nozzle pointed down. Apparently engrossed solely in cleaning it, in order to make it create a good suction, he proceeded to squeeze the pump again and again. I heard the sharp wheeze and saw the tube, quite accidentally, it seemed, even to me, pointed at Heregrove's legs. Mr. Mycroft still shook the apparatus, almost straightening himself in the effort, and evidently so engrossed in getting it into working order that he did not notice that it was still pointed at Heregrove and now was actually in line with his body. Heregrove stood still, impatiently waiting for what he took to be a small air-suction pump to be brought into working order.

"*There* it is," said Mr. Mycroft, stooping again. "That's right. Now it is drawing. Only the slightest snuff does it, once it's working. Pollens are a wonderful study. Specks almost invisible to the eye, each has its very distinctive shape, telling you what genus it belongs to, giving you the whole history of a plant—indeed, with these wonderful fossil pollens, the whole ancestry of genera and orders of plants. But not the plant's copyright, in this case. So you are safe, Mr. Heregrove, from our taking anything from you even unintentionally. Our task in coming here," he continued, a less rambling manner coming into his speech, "was to make you an offer, an offer, which you, on due consideration, refused."

He straightened up. Suddenly the old flower enthusiast completely dropped from him, as a mound of ivy at a stroke may be stripped off and leave visible a gaunt tower which it has concealed.

"Good night, Mr. Heregrove, good night, and if in the night you should—I have done so myself and have found such thoughts well deserving my prompt action—wake and reconsider your decision, I do pray that you will come straight down to me without a moment's delay. I should really be grateful, more grateful than perhaps I can make you understand, if you could see your way to take the line I have been able to suggest. I know I must seem to you an absurd old man, fanatically fussing about what isn't his business and, you may even think, pleading with sentimental urgency for the protection and preservation of a queer and outwardly not important variety of life's many manifestations and mysterious forms. Is it worth, you think, being so particular? Why trouble to preserve everything that wants to live? Are things so important? Believe me, it is not the cash nor the reputation which I feel to be at stake. All life needs protection, encouragement, defense. We can't be indifferent or ruthless, can we?"

He trailed off rather lamely, and I was glad enough. Heregrove's patience was at an end. No shadow yet passed over his assurance that we were in his power, nor he by any possibility in ours. He turned rudely on his heel.

"I've wasted more time than I can spare," he remarked over his shoulder. "Shut the gate as you go out."

He swung off down the path toward the fields. Mr. Mycroft said nothing. I followed him as he walked swiftly past the house, reached the gate, opened it, carefully relatched it, and went down the road.

9

FLY BREAKS FROM WASP

HE KEPT silence until we were at my gate. Then he turned to me.

"I hope you did not mind being likened, together with myself, to a tulip of an odd variety. After all, the greatest poets have thought our lives are closely similar in their fates to the grasses of the field; and we have been asked by a high authority to consider each other, among other reasons, because of the moving, transitory beauty of flower life." Then, more gravely, "I had to give him every chance; even to taking that considerable risk at the end. I had to count on his dismissing as a chance coincidence (though the wise know there is no chance in life) that my concern for the plant's life and his indifference to it, pointed to, was a parable of, his terrible indifference to human life. I hoped this queer illustration might awaken him. It was a last hope. For a moment I suspected that he wondered whether I was aware of how apposite my words were in his case. But he is too sunk in that brutal self-assurance which is the final and fatal ignorance, that ignorance, that ignoring of appeal and warning which the most merciful and wisest of all the religions, Buddhism, rightly calls the chief and the one unforgivable sin. At least in this life. And that is all we poor men of action can provide for. The lesser of two evils here—and the hope that elsewhere, under other conditions, those who have found this life and body only a noose in which their struggles of greed and fear strangle them and make them in their blind strivings only a peril to all near them, may awake to their illusion, it may drop from them like an evil dream and they begin again to live and understand."

He was evidently moved, and though I was naturally disinclined to follow his rather extravagant speculations, I was quite distinctly willing that he should run on. I did not want to be left alone. The tension of action was over. I had come away from the drama. The curtain had gone down on the act. Now we had to wait on Destiny. My mind was being blown about, now that I was having time to reflect. I felt that, left to myself, I should hardly sleep and, if I did, my dreams all too easily might be worse than any wakeful worrying, however weary. I felt that I must retain Mr. Mycroft and keep him in my company by some means. It struck me that he might stay a little longer if I asked him to clear up a few points which in the last few hours I had failed to understand fully. Of course I had followed his main strategy, but certain details of his tactics had escaped me. I was too tired really to be interested, but I saw that by asking him to explain, his delight in showing one how clever he was would keep him hanging about and save me a little longer from the solitude which I now dreaded.

"I didn't quite follow," I said, in as abstract a voice as I could command, "some particulars of your behavior in the garden. Of course I grasped the main drift, but all that play with the paper, the letter, which I suppose must have been a sham?"

"Yet," he replied with a patience which would normally have irritated me but now was a relief, guaranteeing me a little longer human company, "yet you saw every step of those preparations. You saw me go to the door and come back with a piece of letter paper printed with official headings, a piece of official stationery, and you had every reason to arrive by induction at the fact that I had had that piece of stationery specially prepared for the work we had on hand. You then watched me while I took out a similar sheet, but with writing on it and, with the sheet I had had prepared turned upside down, you saw me copy something. Again, what, and what alone, could such an action convey?"

He paused, but I was not trying to think, only to keep his company.

"I gave you," he continued, when he saw that I was going to say nothing, "the full explanation while I talked to Heregrove. My actions could mean only one thing. I was copying, from a letter, which I had had from him, Dr. Miles's signature, and, of course, like all copyists or forgers of signatures or handwriting, I copied it upside down. That is the only safe way of preventing tricks of one's own handwriting from appearing in the letters and words which you wish to render facsimile. I didn't expect that Heregrove would know Miles's signature. But nothing must be left unprovided for and he might have seen it. If he had (for, as I said, that sign-manual is a remarkable exhibition of nervous vigor and display, if not of calligraphy), then my facsimile would have clinched his conviction that we were harmless. Only under a strong glass would suspicion be wakened, for then, as in all such slowly 'drawn' characters, instead of one or two small wobbles appearing at intervals on the dozen or so strokes, there would be visible quite a number of such regularly occurring little jolts in the lines. That fact has often caught forgers. These jolts are the records of the heart-beats. If you take half a minute to copy a signature and only a couple of seconds or so to write it if it is your own, you see, these tell-tale marks, giving your time and showing your amount of labor, must be much more frequent in the copy. But I took care to bring away the letter—you heard me type it after I had signed it—and I shall burn it now when I get home. I must be going. There are a number of such small things to do this evening."

I felt that I must make a straightforward attempt to hold him; just asking questions could no longer stave off my being left alone.

"I wonder," I said hesitatingly, "I wonder whether you would be so kind, Mr. Mycroft, as to stay with me tonight?"

"I am afraid that would not be wise," he answered kindly. "As I have said, I must clear up a few things at home, which you will recall need tidying up."

I understood. There was not merely the letter. The flask was still in his pocket and Mr. Mycroft, believing as he did in Destiny, left nothing to "chance." He hesitated.

"I would ask you to come to my place but, again, the less we are seen about together, the better, at least at present. In a village a recluse cannot change his ways and make friends without people asking why he has done so and even what enmity has driven him to seek allies! After all, do what we will, our neighbors are always forming opinions about us, and if we for a long time do not see any reason why we should care, we may be sure that the stories they tell about us will be more to their fancy than to ours."

"All right," I said, with a sudden, tired petulance. "All

right. I am the most exposed. Nearer the danger; next on the list; leave me to face it alone."

All my restraint had gone I could not think where, but as I spoke the very words seemed to carry away that last crust of assurance and restraint. Mr. Mycroft's face was hard to see in the late summer dusk. His face was as difficult to estimate.

"You have gone through your ordeal and now you are in the reaction," said the even tones. "It would be wise not to fall into ignorance about your condition. It was not your normal self which carried you through today. Our lives would have been forfeit if I had taken the risk of depending on such power as you have at your command to make yourself behave reliably. I saw and studied your reaction to benzedrine hydrate. Like many of your type, you are extremely responsive to certain drugs. I therefore gave you temporarily the Batavian bravery which is not yours by nature. Now you must pay the cost in reaction. Perhaps not an exorbitant fee, considering that it is the only one charged for saving your life."

It maddened me that this old man had played with me, treating me as an equal while all the time he was only doping me like a race horse and forcing me into acts which I already saw had made me exchange the *possibility* of a danger, which anyhow was growing less (after all, who knows, as the first attack had failed, I might never be set on again), for a far graver one which well might dog me all my life. And then the complete disregard of my feelings, to speak to me in that insolent way when he owned I was tired out. Not the slightest attempt to make things easy for me, but a lecture which an old, angry schoolmaster might give a child before caning it.

"Good night, Mr. Mycroft," I said, sharply. I left him standing, slammed my gate, got into my house, went straight upstairs, and was safe in my bedroom before the energy given me by my outburst and the relief of being rude had worn off and I felt even worse.

I remembered that I had had no supper and it was quite time for it. But I couldn't even face going down to the larder. I felt that I should see Heregrove's face peering at me through the wire-gauze window. I took a warm bath, but the rushing of the taps made me dread I should not hear if there should come a step on the stairs. At last I was in bed, but if I have ever had a worse night I don't remember it.

When the light came, however, as so often happens, so provokingly, I did fall asleep. I woke, therefore, late, exhausted and vexed at hearing the disturbing noise Alice was making below. She might realize that this morning of all mornings, I reflected, I might be left, as she would say, to sleep it out. And then I realized that she could never know, must never know, must never have a suggestion of a suspicion. I must always be bright and cheerful and on time, for fear she and then others might begin to remark on how changed I was, how moping now: "Looks like he never slept a wink"; "And all since those days when he was all about with that queer Mr. Mycroft"; "Well, birds of a feather . . ."; "An you know that was exactly the time when he fancied himself into a fit over bees!"

I flung myself out of bed, pounding down heavily on the floor. Alice would thus know I was up and full of energy. I splashed about in the bath—that, too, would show vitality and also give her plenty to do mopping up and polishing down—lack of work makes gossips. Then downstairs, making, I thought, a pretty good entry as an active, rested man, ready to take up his own interests and business and able to tell others to mind theirs.

But Alice was evidently not impressed. In fact, she didn't seem to notice my carefully prepared carriage and poise. She was full of something else and, alas, I knew it, before she began: "Pore"—I must own the "dear" was omitted, but the "pore," like a code-word, told me all. Yes, the milkman, she'd seen him herself as she'd been coming along and it was he who had found Heregrove. Stiff already, halfway up the garden path. Had called "Milk, O," and Mr. Heregrove (disaster, I could not help noticing, had given him a "Mister"), who was always early, hadn't answered. So Alf had thrown a glance up the garden path. Couldn't b'lieve his eyes; why, black he was as the earth he lay on.

"Alice," I said, "would you please make my bedroom now? I may have caught a chill and will probably go back to bed after breakfast."

She left the room with that stiff rapidity which indicates deep offense. I had cut her off retailing first-class news. She, the semi-sacred bearer of almost first-hand evil tidings, was silenced. Well, at least she did not suspect how horribly prepared I had been for her news. I did go back to bed after breakfast. I wanted to lie and think undisturbed. It was clear that Heregrove was dead. I was safe. But the clearer it became that he was gone, the more tenuous seemed the risk which I had run while he was alive and the darker loomed the possible danger which I must now watch rise and hang over me—perhaps never to be dissipated—certainly beyond the power of any private, well-meaning, but really busy-bodying old gentleman to deliver me from.

About noon there was a ring at the bell. Alice knocked and entered with a look of muted triumph which at once added to my misgivings.

"Please, sir, Bob Withers, the policeman, would like to see you for a moment."

I went downstairs, my heart sinking at every step. The village constable is not an awe-inspiring functionary. This one was as nervous as I, which was saying a great deal then. He had taken off his helmet and was passing it from one hand to the other, as though it were hot. He certainly was. After our mumbled good-mornings, he broke his message. It was about that there Mr. Heregrove. Perhaps I'd heard, perhaps not, but he was in the mortuary and as (here was the point) I had last been seen with him, it was wondered whether I could 'elp showing 'ow 'e came to his Hend.

It was preposterous that they should come to me when Mr. Mycroft had actually planned the visit and— but I must not ever even let my mind finish that sentence! Anyhow, I simply could not go through this alone. Only a little while ago in this abominable affair, I had foreseen myself driven into the lunatic asylum for life; now even such an end seemed an escape, a refuge, considering the alternative place where it seemed that a single slip of the tongue, a single thought aloud, would land me with—the best I could hope for—a life sentence!

My mind moved quickly, but I think my tongue was even quicker, for I heard myself saying, "Mr. Mycroft, of Waller's Lane, and I did visit Mr. Heregrove last evening. He had supplied us with honey. We spent a few minutes with him in his garden. He seemed quite well then."

"Oh, if Mr. Mycroft was with you, sir, perhaps you'd come along of me while I get is statement, too."

I saw that was quite the best thing in the bad circumstances and agreed. However much I did not want
to see the old man, a time had come when he must carry
us out of our common difficulty. It was his, really, more
than mine, and anything which that cunning old brain
planned to cover its own self and tracks would cover
mine too.

On reaching his house we found him on his lawn.
I felt as though he had been expecting us. He certainly showed no surprise, and nodded silently when Bob
Withers told him that Heregrove had been discovered
dead. We did not know whether he had heard the news
before or not, and when asked for a statement, he simply remarked that he had seen the deceased the evening
before and thought he seemed well.

Then he added, "I know, constable, you would like
us to go with you to the magistrate to whom this case
has been reported. Is it Colonel Treaves? Yes, I thought
it was likely. He is generally on the spot. I can come
along now."

He picked up his hat which was lying on a chair near
him and without a word to me walked along with Withers, I at the constable's other side.

Ten minutes took us to the magistrate's house. We
were shown in at once to his study. A lean, athletic man
of about sixty, I judged, he rose from his chair as we
entered and put out his hand to Mr. Mycroft—he only

nodded to me—saying, "It is kind of you to come over so promptly, sir. Always better to have a direct talk than get statements. But didn't want to trouble you, were you busy at the moment. I was informed that Mr. Silchester here and someone who accompanied him—and I suppose you were that person—last saw this man Heregrove alive?"

"Yes," replied Mr. Mycroft. "We visited him, for he had supplied both Mr. Silchester and myself with honey."

"Well, you probably know," remarked Colonel Treaves, "his bees caught him—like Acteon, wasn't it, and his hounds, what?"

"Do you mean to say that he was attacked by his own hives?" asked Mr. Mycroft, with convincing interest.

"Well, I don't think there can be a shadow of doubt on that point. You may not know—think it was before you came to the village—but his wretched wife died the same way and the coroner then told him to have the bees destroyed. He said he would, too. He either disobeyed the court's order or the Heregroves must have had something about them that bees can't stand. Never liked either of them myself—and the man! Well, *nisi bonum*. He was certainly stung to death; the body is swollen and black as a ripe mulberry."

That made me feel quite sick.

"All I would like to ask you gentlemen," he continued, "is whether, when you called on him, he seemed well and in a normal frame of mind?"

"Oh, yes," replied Mr. Mycroft. "I thought he was a queer customer and he was obviously a bit of a recluse, but he was certainly sane and healthy when we saw him, wasn't he, Mr. Silchester?"

"Oh, quite, quite," was all I could say, and all it seemed that I was expected to say.

"We took a turn or two with him in his garden," went on Mr. Mycroft. "It was impossible to judge on what terms he was with his bees, for they had retired for the evening. Perhaps we ran more of a risk than seemed apparent by calling on a man who was in such peril."

"Perhaps so, perhaps so," answered the colonel. "You never can tell. Bees are certainly queer beasts. In India I have known fifty people going down a lane. Suddenly from the sky will drop what seems a cloud of dust. It's a swarm of small, savage, forest bees. The swarm'll slump on one poor fellow, leaving unvisited everyone else. If there isn't a pool handy for him to be flung into, he may be dead in a few minutes and swollen like Heregrove's body. Some people say it's smell, but I don't believe anyone really knows. In India we say Bismillah—Allah's Will, and, after all, everything ends there finally."

10

AS WE WERE?

AND THERE, to my surprise, our fantastic mixture of adventure and persecution, of gratuitous attack and undetected counterattack, of scientific planning and Wild-West justice, came to an end. As suddenly as this typhoon had blown across the quiet track of my life, as suddenly it dropped. I live now in what I can only call a suspicious hush. We attended, more as honored guests than as summoned witnesses, the coroner's court. The coroner took the same view as the magistrate, with the added animus of, "Serve him right, disobeying my instructions." He also ordered, with the pointless pleasure to himself of just exercising authority, but to my keen though concealed delight, the destruction of the Heregrove hives.

As we left the court, Mr. Mycroft, who had, till now, abstained from speaking to me, strolled along at my side until the small crowd had dissipated itself. Then he remarked quietly, "Unpleasant associations are not the best foundation for an acquaintance, but an adventure shared sometimes is. I realize that you have had many shocks during these days and that once or twice I had to push you harder than you found agreeable, if we were not to be caught in the Caudine Forks, with results which would have been disastrous. I think now, however, you will realize that the wood is behind, the pursuers are scattered."

He seemed complacently assured. Perhaps it was the wish to find some adequate excuse for resenting his complacency and coolness, neither of which I could myself feel, that made me reply, "But what about our actual position? After all, whether we were really in such grave danger as we thought we can never be certain."

He looked as though he were going to interrupt, but I was determined to have my say out. Not only had I been treated like a child throughout this whole affair, as though I could not be expected to have a clear judgment on matters which did concern me more than anyone else, but when we went to see Colonel Treaves I had been hurt at the way both men had behaved, again, as though I were a child. Now I would assert my rights and he should hear my considered opinion.

"What we can be sure of," I continued, "is that we threw off what we took to be our pursuer by throwing him to his death. He may, at the worst, have intended to do no more than scare us. We certainly killed him. It is, I know, a nasty word, but it is better out and off my mind."

Mr. Mycroft allowed himself a short sigh.

"No law in any country," he said, slowly, "and I know something of the rules which men have made in attempting to save the innocent and helpless from the ruthless strong—no law would have given a cruel and calculating murderer the chances I gave him or would authorize the running of those risks which I took in order that he should have every opportunity, in fact, even a bribe, to turn him from his course. He was, you will remember, already a murderer and I was prepared, rather than take the line which all human justice has decreed, to treat his horrible, patiently-worked-out crime as a slip, as a bygone to be treated as something which had not taken place and not—as, alas, mankind is right in judging—as the fruit, and only the first fruit, of a long-nourished and now richly yielding root of evil.

"The Romans with their legal minds were correct. I quoted the Latin judgment that day when we were discussing the evolution of venom in animals. It is certainly as true of us: *Nemo repente fuit turpissimus*, the murderer ripens more slowly than the saint—both are not accidents but achievements. Heregrove could not turn from his way, at the point where he crossed our path, even if the past were to be blotted out and the present to offer him a prize if he would only abstain from turning bloodshed into a business. He needed someone to bring home his crime to him, and that we could not do. We could only offer to deflect him. He would have gone on the same way in other fields."

I broke in there. "But your offer was a sham!" I exclaimed.

It was the only time I saw Mr. Mycroft nearly angry. His face didn't change color or the expression alter, but I caught sight of some slight alteration in his eyes which I own made me positively scared. Somehow I had never thought of him as someone who might be fearsome. Helpful, amusing, irritating, managing, boring—yes, all these things, but never formidable. Yet that gleam—I can't call it a flash—was certainly very disconcerting. It seemed not so much as though one were looking at a man whom I was trying to provoke and who I suddenly realized, might strike back at me, but rather that I was suddenly looking through a porthole, through the eyeholes of a mask out onto something as cold, impersonal, and indifferent as an iceberg emerging from a mist and seen bearing down on my ship.

"I mean," I rather stammered, "the letter was a fake. There was no offer for Heregrove, as a matter of fact, to accept?"

"You think then, that I did not really plead with that

wretched man, caught in the toils of his own evil thought which had set until it became evil deed? Did not seek to make it possible, if it might be, that he should break out of his self-made trap? That I simply mocked him, pretending to hold out a helping hand and point a way out of the false dilemma he had caught and impaled his conscience on: 'Murder or starve'? That I put on a piece of play-acting the better to amuse myself and you with an exposition of the skill with which I had trapped and deluded a fellow creature, even though he was our enemy and mankind's?"

"Well," I protested, with my heart, I must confess, beating quite unpleasantly, for he was driving me onto the defensive when I had been sure I had a case against him. "Well, he could not have taken an opportunity which actually was quite fictitious."

"The offer," replied Mr. Mycroft gravely, "had to be—as are all life's offers—in a form in which he could believe and could, if there were no wish in him to serve Life and not Death, refuse. Do you suppose he would have been more likely and more able to accept had I said, 'You are, of course, a murderer whom the law cannot convict or even recognize. You are now planning to murder us and God knows how many more. If you will abstain I will pay you three or four hundred pounds and get you out of your financial embarrassments'?"

Mr. Mycroft waited a moment, but I was dogged. He

was certainly putting his dreadful and very awkward deed in a very clear light.

"Still," I replied, "I am sorry to appear stubborn and to be precise. The real fact that remains, when all is said, is that he could not have been given the alternative to which you verbally urged him."

"I am sorry," answered Mr. Mycroft—and I was alarmed to hear come into his voice actually something of that very same tone which I had heard when Heregrove refused the offer which we were now discussing and Mr. Mycroft used those same words with a curious, ominous conviction.

"Mr. Silchester, I am sorry that we have seen so much of each other and you are yet capable of thinking that I would lie to a man in mortal peril, offering him a spurious escape. As I have said, I could not tell him from whence in actual fact would come the resources which I guaranteed for his deliverance, would he but accept and turn, if only for a moment, from his way. We were his prey. Even if he could have faced the fact that we knew he was a murderer, he could not have believed in our *bona fides*. Man imputes himself. The fact that we were in possession of such knowledge he could only interpret as his nature could understand—that we would for the rest of his life do as he would do to such another who should fall into *his* power—blackmail him. Add to that fact that we come to offer him money, not immediately to extort it, and he can only be the more certain that here is a doubly cunning trap, beside which blackmail is aboveboard business. No; the disguise of form was essential for his one chance of safety, even more than for ours. But the substance, the firm offer was there.

"Because I have learned that expression of emotion is mere sentimentality, Mr. Silchester, I must ask you to believe that that certainly does not mean that I am without feelings, still less coolly irresponsible. By every possible means, I was determined to rescue that murderer and to spare him from the fate he was drawing on himself, if I could. I was as set on that as on saving *your* life at the cost of compelling you more than once to act, when you would much have preferred to procrastinate and dally.

"The offer made Heregrove was a real one. I had arranged that, should he go to the address I would name and which I should see he would think was that of the registered offices and the legal adviser of the Society where he would receive his grant-in-aid, he should be received by a long-trusted solicitor friend of mine, given £200 with his ticket and any other expenses paid to any place he should choose to go, and with a firm offer of another £200 when he arrived at his destination. My friend was to be sufficiently (but not too fully) seized of the case, being told that Heregrove was a blackmailer against whom a charge would be difficult to present and who should be given this chance of clearing out. This friend of mine, as have many fine solicitors in the course of their practice, has dealt across his quiet, brief-covered table with more than one such dangerous man in this effective way. What the large forceps of the law cannot pick up and must leave lurking under our feet, often the steady hand of a wise solicitor can lay hold of and drop out of the window. The plan would have worked, had Heregrove assented, for I have so broken the news—if I may use that phrase—to several unconvictable criminals, that I knew their record and would give them one more chance, and quite a number have made good. But Heregrove was by nature not one of these. I repeat the question, and must ask you to reply, 'Was not he self-doomed?'"

He was right, just, and generous, I had to allow, but still I could say nothing. This last display of such courageous, thoughtful efficiency, I know, ought to have swept away my last timid considerations and have made me apologize as handsomely as possible, urged by a not less generous trustfulness. Awkward as it was for me to recognize, I could no longer avoid seeing—indeed, I had forced him to prove to me—that he was a wonder, a man ahead of his age in skill and also in justice. His attempt to save the murderer was no less wonderful, patient, and daring than his success in saving the designated murderee.

Yet, somehow, the very supermanly quality about it all put me off, daunted me. I don't want to have to live with mental or moral geniuses. They may always be expecting you to be heroic, and he certainly had landed me in a position which might quite easily at any moment become dangerous.

"I don't know," I said. "I really don't know. I shall never be sure. Right or wrong, the thing, as it has actually happened, or been made to happen, will always be hanging over me. It might at any time come out, and then in spite of all the fine motives which I don't doubt prompted the actual deed, where shall we be, what will be my position?"

He looked at me again as though he were making up his mind whether to say more or no, whether to tell me something further or to leave things as they were. As I did not believe that there was any answer to my question and so felt pretty hopeless about the whole matter, I really didn't care whether he went on trying to console me, or left me alone. Evidently he decided, in the end, that he could do something for me.

"As to your position," he said, "I think I can reassure you by telling you one more thing. It, too, is a secret. Mycroft is only one of my family names."

I could not help wondering, on hearing this opening, to what fresh freak of vanity I was to be introduced.

This sudden emphasis upon himself showed how his egotism had to peep out even when the matter in hand was my safety. How could his family names matter to me, much less protect me? We were not in the Middle Ages and he a big baron.

"I have used Mycroft," he complacently continued, "because my full name was once pretty widely known, and I wanted, when I retired, to be quiet and unmolested. You have been served, and, I may add, if you so wish, you are still under the protection" (the man seemed quite self-assured that I should so wish)—"your case still has as its defense—"

There! I have forgotten the name he gave himself. It was something not unlike Mycroft—Mycroft and then another word, a short one, I think. But I was too bothered to memorize still another set of names, especially as it was quite clear that they could really be no defense to me. I had known him as Mycroft, had known both his capacities and limitations. I could not see how the one would become the greater or the other less by calling him by another name. As Mycroft we had struggled along together through this upsetting business. I suppose he or Destiny had got me out, but only at the cost of leaving me under an abiding apprehension. I could not feel that there was anything magical in either of his names. It came over me again, and this time with complete conviction, after seeing this last proof of what he thought to be adequate defense, that if I were ever to be safe I would be safer and more comfortable by myself.

"Thank you, Mr. ——"; I think I called him by the new name he evidently so much prized, but which awoke no meaning or association in my mind. "Thank you. I am obliged, and you must forgive what may seem perhaps an apparent churlishness. But I think I will again retire into my shell."

He took my breakaway, I am glad to say, with composure. We were parting without a scene, and I was grateful for that.

"Very well," was all he said.

I thought, then, that perhaps I ought not to leave it quite there but might give some sort of explanation of my action, of why I could not think our continued alliance would add to my safety.

"You see," I said, "now that I do know your real name, I have to own I have never heard of you before."

Then, I must own, he looked amazed—perhaps the only time I had seen him profoundly surprised, and he turned away without a word.

For a moment I felt an immense relief. The feeling grew. I had not anyone to interfere with me any more. I was once more my own master. The relief lasted a couple of days. Then the other darker shadow, the shadow of apprehension, that I was an accessory to murder, if only to counter-murder, settled down on me. That is why I have been driven to write all this. If the worst comes to the worst, after all, Mycroft did it, not I.

Charlotte Armstrong
The Unsuspected

Introduction by Otto Penzler

To catch a murderous theater impresario, a young woman takes a deadly new role...

The note discovered beside Rosaleen Wright's hanged body is full of reasons justifying her suicide—but it lacks her trademark vitality and wit, and, most importantly, her signature. So the note alone is far from enough to convince her best friend Jane that Rosaleen was her own murderer, even if the police quickly accept the possibility as fact. Instead, Jane suspects Rosaleen's boss, Luther Grandison. To the world at large, he's a powerful and charismatic figure, directing for stage and screen, but Rosaleen's letters to Jane described a duplicitous, greedy man who would no doubt kill to protect his secrets. Jane and her friend Francis set out to infiltrate Grandy's world and collect evidence, employing manipulation, impersonation, and even gaslighting to break into his inner circle. But will they recognize what dangers lie therein before it's too late?

CHARLOTTE ARMSTRONG (1905-1969) was an American author of mystery short stories and novels. Having started her writing career as a poet and dramatist, she wrote a few novels before *The Unsuspected*, which was her first to achieve outstanding success going on to be adapted for film by Michael Curtiz.

"Psychologically rich, intricately plotted and full of dark surprises, Charlotte Armstrong's suspense tales feel as vivid and fresh today as a half century ago."
—Megan Abbott

Paperback, $15.95 / ISBN 978-1-61316-123-4
Hardcover, $25.95 / ISBN 978-1-61316-122-7

Erle Stanley Gardner
The Case of the
Careless Kitten

Introduction by Otto Penzler

Perry Mason seeks the link between a poisoned kitten and a mysterious voice from the past

Soon after Helen Kendal receives a mysterious phone call from her vanished uncle Franklin, long presumed dead, urging her to make contact with criminal defense attorney Perry Mason, she finds herself the main suspect in the murder of an unfamiliar man. Her kitten has just survived a poisoning attempt—as has her aunt Matilda, who always maintained that Franklin was alive in spite of his disappearance. Certain of his client's innocence, Mason gets to work outwitting the police to solve the crime; to do so, he'll enlist the help of his secretary Della Street, his private eye Paul Drake, and the unlikely but invaluable aid of a careless but very clever kitten.

ERLE STANLEY GARDNER (1889-1970) was the best-selling American author of the 20th century, mainly due to the enormous success of his Perry Mason series. For more than a quarter of a century he wrote more than a million words a year under his own name and numerous pseudonyms, the most famous being A.A. Fair. His series books can be read in any order.

"[Erle Stanley Gardner's] Mason books remain tantalizing on every page and brilliant."
—Scott Turow

Paperback, $15.95 / ISBN 978-1-61316-116-6
Hardcover, $25.95 / ISBN 978-1-61316-115-9

Dorothy B. Hughes
The So Blue Marble

Introduction by Otto Penzler

Three well-heeled villains terrorize New York's high society in pursuit of a rare and powerful gem

The society pages announce it before she even arrives: Griselda Satterlee, daughter of the princess of Rome, has left her career as an actress behind and is traveling to Manhattan to reinvent herself as a fashion designer. They also announce the return of the dashing Montefierrow twins to New York after a twelve-year sojourn in Europe. But there is more to this story than what's reported: The twins are seeking a rare and powerful gem they believe to be stashed in the unused apartment where Griselda is staying, and they won't take no for an answer. When they return, accompanied by Griselda's long-estranged younger sister, the murders begin... Drenched in the glamour and luxury of the New York elite, *The So Blue Marble* is a perfectly Art Deco suspense novel in which nothing is quite as it seems.

DOROTHY B. HUGHES (1904–1993) was a mystery author and literary critic. Several of her novels were adapted for film, including *In a Lonely Place* and *Ride the Pink Horse*, and in 1978, the Mystery Writers of America presented her with the Grand Master Award.

"Readers new to this forgotten classic are in for a treat."—*Publishers Weekly*

Paperback, $15.95 / ISBN 978-1-61316-105-0

Hardcover, $25.95 / ISBN 978-1-61316-111-1

OTTO PENZLER PRESENTS
AMERICAN MYSTERY CLASSICS

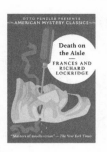

Frances & Richard Lockridge
Death on the Aisle
A Mr. & Mrs. North Mystery

Introduction by Otto Penzler

Broadway may be a graveyard of hopes and dreams, but someone's adding corpses to its tombs...

Mr. and Mrs. North live as quiet a life as a couple can amidst the bustle of New York City. For Jerry, a publisher, and Pamela, a homemaker, the only threat to their domestic equilibrium comes in the form of Mrs. North's relentless efforts as an amateur sleuth, which repeatedly find the duo investigating crimes. So when the wealthy backer of a play is found dead in the seats of the West 45th Street Theatre, the Norths aren't far behind, led by Pam's customary flair for murders that turn eccentric and, yes, humorous. A light mystery set in a classic Broadway locale, *Death on the Aisle* is the fourth novel and one of the best in the saga of this charming, witty couple, which can be enjoyed in any order.

FRANCES AND RICHARD LOCKRIDGE were two of the most popular names in mystery during the forties and fifties, collaborating to write twenty-six mystery novels about the Mr. & Mrs. North couple, which, in turn, became the subject of a Broadway play, a movie, and series for both radio and television.

"Masters of misdirection."
—The New York Times

Paperback, $15.95 / ISBN 978-1-61316-118-0
Hardcover, $25.95 / ISBN 978-1-61316-117-3

OTTO PENZLER PRESENTS
===AMERICAN MYSTERY CLASSICS===

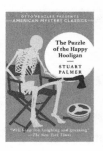

Stuart Palmer
The Puzzle of the
Happy Hooligan

Introduction by Otto Penzler

*After a screenwriter is murdered on a film set, a
street-smart school teacher searches for the killer*

Hildegarde Withers is just your average school teacher—with above-average skills in the art of deduction. The New Yorker often finds herself investigating crimes led only by her own meddlesome curiosity, though her friends on the NYPD don't mind when she solves their cases for them. After plans for a grand tour of Europe are interrupted by Germany's invasion of Poland, Miss Withers heads to sunny Los Angeles instead, where her vacation finds her working as a technical advisor on the set of a film adaptation of the Lizzie Borden story. The producer has plans for an epic retelling of the historical killer's patricidal spree—plans which are derailed when a screenwriter turns up dead. While the local authorities quickly deem his death accidental, Withers suspects otherwise and calls up a detective back home for advice. The two soon team up to catch a wily killer.

STUART PALMER (1905–1968) was an American author of mysteries. Born in Baraboo, Wisconsin, Palmer worked a number of odd jobs—including apple picking, journalism, and copywriting—before publishing his first novel, the crime drama *Ace of Jades*, in 1931.

"Will keep you laughing and guessing from the first page to the last."—*The New York Times*

Paperback, $15.95 / ISBN 978-1-61316-104-3

Hardcover, $25.95 / ISBN 978-1-61316-114-2

Ellery Queen
The Dutch Shoe Mystery

Introduction by Otto Penzler

After a wealthy woman is strangled in a hospital full of friends, Ellery Queen seeks her deadly enemy

When millionaire and philanthropist Abigail Doorn falls into a coma, she is taken to the hospital she funds for an emergency operation at the hands of her protégé, one of the leading surgeons on the East Coast. Her friends and family flock to the scene, anxious to hear of the outcome; also in attendance is mystery writer and amateur detective Ellery Queen, invited by a member of the hospital staff. Covered in a white sheet, her form is wheeled into the main operating theater—but when the sheet is pulled back, it reveals a grim display: the garroted corpse of the patient, murdered before the chance at survival. Who among the attendees was ruthless enough to carry out this gruesome act? As the list of suspects grows, and the murders continue, it's up to Queen—and the most perceptive of readers—to uncover the clues and find out.

ELLERY QUEEN was a pen name created and shared by two cousins, Frederic Dannay (1905-1982) and Manfred B. Lee (1905-1971), as well as the name of their most famous detective. Born in Brooklyn, they spent forty-two years writing the greatest puzzle-mysteries of their time, gaining the duo a reputation as the foremost American authors of the Golden Age "fair play" mystery.

"Ellery Queen *is* the American detective story."
—Anthony Boucher

Paperback, $15.95 / ISBN 978-1-61316-127-2
Hardcover, $25.95 / ISBN 978-1-61316-126-5

Ellery Queen
The Chinese Orange Mystery

Introduction by Otto Penzler

A topsy-turvy crime scene sends Ellery Queen on a puzzling quest for the truth

The offices of foreign literature publisher and renowned stamp collector Donald Kirk are often host to strange activities, but the most recent occurrence—the murder of an unknown caller, found dead in an empty waiting room—is unlike any that has come before. Nobody, it seems, entered or exited the room, and yet the crime scene clearly has been manipulated, leaving everything in the room turned backwards and upside down. Stuck through the back of the corpse's shirt are two long spears—and a tangerine is missing from the fruit bowl. Enter amateur sleuth Ellery Queen, who arrives just in time to witness the discovery of the body, only to be immediately drawn into a complex case in which no clue is too minor or too glaring to warrant careful consideration.

ELLERY QUEEN was a pen name created and shared by two cousins, Frederic Dannay (1905-1982) and Manfred B. Lee (1905-1971), as well as the name of their most famous detective. Born in Brooklyn, they spent forty-two years writing the greatest puzzle-mysteries of their time, gaining the duo a reputation as the foremost American authors of the Golden Age "fair play" mystery.

"Without doubt the best of the Queen stories."—*The New York Times*

Paperback, $15.95 / ISBN 978-1-61316-106-7
Hardcover, $25.95 / ISBN 978-1-61316-110-4

Patrick Quentin
A Puzzle for Fools

Introduction by Otto Penzler

*A wave of murders rocks a sanitarium
—and it's up to the patients to stop them*

Broadway producer Peter Duluth sought solace in a bottle after his wife's death; now, two years later and desperate to dry out, he enters a sanitarium, hoping to break his dependence on drink—but the institution doesn't quite offer the rest and relaxation he expected. Strange, malevolent occurrences plague the hospital; among other inexplicable events, Peter hears his own voice with an ominous warning: "There will be murder." It soon becomes clear that a homicidal maniac is on the loose and, with a staff every bit as erratic as its idiosyncratic patients, it seems everyone is a suspect—even Duluth's new romantic interest, Iris Pattison. Charged by the head of the ward with solving the crimes, it's up to Peter to clear her name before the killer strikes again.

PATRICK QUENTIN is one pseudonym of Hugh Callingham Wheeler (1912-1987), born in London, who eventually became a US citizen. Writing in collaboration with a revolving cast of co-authors under the Quentin, Q. Patrick and Jonathan Stagge names, Wheeler produced more than 30 mystery novels. He later gravitated to the stage and wrote, among other plays, the Tony award-winning *Sweeney Todd*.

"Mr. Quentin is a craftsman of the first class."
—Times Literary Supplement

Paperback, $15.95 / ISBN 978-1-61316-125-8
Hardcover, $25.95 / ISBN 978-1-61316-124-1

Clayton Rawson
Death From a Top Hat

Introduction by Otto Penzler

A detective steeped in the art of magic solves the mystifying murder of two occultists

Now retired from the tour circuit on which he made his name, master magician The Great Merlini spends his days running a magic shop in New York's Times Square and his nights moonlighting as a consultant for the NYPD. The cops call him when faced with crimes so impossible that they can only be comprehended by a magician's mind. In the most recent case, two occultists are discovered dead in locked rooms, one spread out on a pentagram, both appearing to have been murdered under similar circumstances. The list of suspects includes an escape artist, a professional medium, and a ventriloquist, so it's clear that the crimes took place in a realm that Merlini knows well. But in the end it will take his logical skills, and not his magical ones, to apprehend the killer.

CLAYTON RAWSON (1906–1971) was a novelist, editor, and magician. He is best known for creating the Great Merlini, an illusionist and amateur sleuth introduced in *Death from a Top Hat* (1938). In 1945 Rawson was among the founders of the Mystery Writers of America; he also served for many years as the editor of *Ellery Queen's Mystery Magazine*.

"One of the all-time greatest impossible murder mysteries."—*Publishers Weekly*

Paperback, $15.95 / ISBN 978-1-61316-101-2
Hardcover, $25.95 / ISBN 978-1-61316-109-8

Patrick Quentin
A Puzzle for Fools

Introduction by Otto Penzler

A wave of murders rocks a sanitarium —and it's up to the patients to stop them

Broadway producer Peter Duluth sought solace in a bottle after his wife's death; now, two years later and desperate to dry out, he enters a sanitarium, hoping to break his dependence on drink—but the institution doesn't quite offer the rest and relaxation he expected. Strange, malevolent occurrences plague the hospital; among other inexplicable events, Peter hears his own voice with an ominous warning: "There will be murder." It soon becomes clear that a homicidal maniac is on the loose and, with a staff every bit as erratic as its idiosyncratic patients, it seems everyone is a suspect—even Duluth's new romantic interest, Iris Pattison. Charged by the head of the ward with solving the crimes, it's up to Peter to clear her name before the killer strikes again.

PATRICK QUENTIN is one pseudonym of Hugh Callingham Wheeler (1912-1987), born in London, who eventually became a US citizen. Writing in collaboration with a revolving cast of co-authors under the Quentin, Q. Patrick and Jonathan Stagge names, Wheeler produced more than 30 mystery novels. He later gravitated to the stage and wrote, among other plays, the Tony award-winning *Sweeney Todd*.

"Mr. Quentin is a craftsman of the first class."
—Times Literary Supplement

Paperback, $15.95 / ISBN 978-1-61316-125-8
Hardcover, $25.95 / ISBN 978-1-61316-124-1

Clayton Rawson
Death From a Top Hat

Introduction by Otto Penzler

*A detective steeped in the art of magic solves the
mystifying murder of two occultists*

Now retired from the tour circuit on which he made his name, master magician The Great Merlini spends his days running a magic shop in New York's Times Square and his nights moonlighting as a consultant for the NYPD. The cops call him when faced with crimes so impossible that they can only be comprehended by a magician's mind. In the most recent case, two occultists are discovered dead in locked rooms, one spread out on a pentagram, both appearing to have been murdered under similar circumstances. The list of suspects includes an escape artist, a professional medium, and a ventriloquist, so it's clear that the crimes took place in a realm that Merlini knows well. But in the end it will take his logical skills, and not his magical ones, to apprehend the killer.

CLAYTON RAWSON (1906–1971) was a novelist, editor, and magician. He is best known for creating the Great Merlini, an illusionist and amateur sleuth introduced in *Death from a Top Hat* (1938). In 1945 Rawson was among the founders of the Mystery Writers of America; he also served for many years as the editor of *Ellery Queen's Mystery Magazine*.

"One of the all-time greatest impossible murder mysteries."—*Publishers Weekly*

Paperback, $15.95 / ISBN 978-1-61316-101-2
Hardcover, $25.95 / ISBN 978-1-61316-109-8

Craig Rice
Home Sweet Homicide

Introduction by Otto Penzler

The children of a mystery writer play amateur sleuths and matchmakers

Unoccupied and unsupervised while mother is working, the children of widowed crime writer Marion Carstairs find diversion wherever they can. So when the kids hear gunshots at the house next door, they jump at the chance to launch their own amateur investigation—and after all, why shouldn't they? They know everything the cops do about crime scenes, having read about them in mother's novels. They know what her literary detectives would do in such a situation, how they would interpret the clues and handle witnesses. Plus, if the children solve the puzzle before the cops, it will do wonders for the sales of mother's novels. But this crime scene isn't a game at all; the murder is real and, when its details prove more twisted than anything in mother's fiction, they'll eventually have to enlist Marion's help to sort out the clues. Or is that just part of their plan to hook her up with the lead detective on the case?

CRAIG RICE (1908–1957), born Georgiana Ann Randolph Craig, was an American author of mystery novels, short stories, and screenplays. Rice's writing style was unique in its ability to mix gritty, hard-boiled writing with the entertainment of a screwball comedy.

"A genuine midcentury classic."—*Booklist*

Paperback, $15.95 / ISBN 978-1-61316-103-6

Hardcover, $25.95 / ISBN 978-1-61316-112-8

Mary Robers Rinehart
The Red Lamp

Introduction by Otto Penzler

*A professor tries to stop a murder spree, uncertain
whether the culprit is man or ghost*

An all-around skeptic when it comes to the supernatural, literature professor William Porter gives no credence to claims that Twin Towers, the seaside manor he's just inherited, might be haunted. He finds nothing mysterious about the conditions in which his Uncle Horace died, leaving the property behind; it was a simple case of cardiac arrest, nothing more. Though his wife, more attuned to spiritual disturbance, refuses to occupy the main house, Porter convinces her to spend a summer at the estate and stay in the lodge elsewhere on the grounds. But, not long after they arrive, Porter sees the apparition that the townspeople speak of. And though he isn't convinced that it is a spirit and not a man, Porter knows that, whichever it is, the figure is responsible for the rash of murders—first of sheep, then of people—that breaks out across the countryside. But caught up in the pursuit, Porter risks implicating himself in the very crimes he hopes to solve.

MARY ROBERTS RINEHART (1876-1958) was the most beloved and best-selling mystery writer in America in the first half of the twentieth century.

"Fans of eerie whodunits with a supernatural tinge will relish this reissue."—*Publishers Weekly*

Paperback, $15.95 / ISBN 978-1-61316-102-9
Hardcover, $25.95 / ISBN 978-1-61316-113-5